"What are said.

"I'm not going

He didn't start and Libby got the His jaw was rough and when she tried to kiss him back it was met by a refusal. This was his kiss to her, his mouth said.

His kiss had her hot, right there in the street, the only movement he allowed was her hands to reach for his chest and slide over the cool fabric of his shirt. He let her experience a fraction of what being held by him felt like, then he cruelly removed the pleasure.

She sucked in the summer night air while craving his mouth again.

"Bed," Daniil said.

"I don't..." Libby halted. What had she been about to say? That she didn't want to?

Well, yes, she did.

Since the age of eight, dancing had come first, which had meant self-discipline.

In everything.

How nice to stand here on the brink of making a decision based purely on now, on her own needs and wants right at this moment.

And she did want.

So she chose to say yes when the wisest choice might have been to decline.

"Bed," Libby said, nodding.

Irresistible Russian Tycoons

Sexy, scandalous and impossible to resist!

Daniil, Sev, Nikolai and Roman have come a long way from the Russian orphanage they grew up in. These days, the four sexy tycoons dominate the world's stage—and are just as famed for their prowess between the sheets!

Untamed and untouched by emotion, can these ruthless men find women to redeem them?

You won't want to miss these sizzling Russians in this sensational quartet from *USA TODAY* bestselling author Carol Marinelli— available only from Harlequin Presents!

The Price of His Redemption
December 2015

The Cost of the Forbidden
January 2016

And watch for Nikolai and Roman's stories... coming soon!

Carol Marinelli

—

The Price of His Redemption

ISBN-13: 978-0-373-13391-8

The Price of His Redemption

First North American Publication 2015

Copyright © 2015 by Carol Marinelli

The publisher acknowledges the copyright holder of the additional work:

Christmas at The Chatsfield
Copyright © 2015 by Harlequin Books S.A.

Special thanks and acknowledgment are given to Maisey Yates for her contribution to The Chatsfield series.

This edition published by arrangement with Harlequin Books S.A.

For questions and comments about the quality of this book, please contact us at CustomerService@Harlequin.com.

Printed in U.S.A.

www.Harlequin.com

Carol Marinelli is a Taurus, with Taurus rising, yet still thinks she is a secret Gemini. Originally from England, she now lives in Australia and is a single mother of three. Apart from her children, writing romance and the friendships forged along the way are her passion. She chooses to believe in a happy-ever-after for all and strives for that in her writing.

Books by Carol Marinelli

Harlequin Presents

The Playboy of Puerto Banus
Playing the Dutiful Wife
Heart of the Desert
Innocent Secretary...Accidentally Pregnant

Playboys of Sicily

Sicilian's Shock Proposal
His Sicilian Cinderella

The Chatsfield

Princess's Secret Baby

Alpha Heroes Meet Their Match

The Only Woman to Defy Him
More Precious than a Crown
Protecting the Desert Princess

Empire of the Sands

Banished to the Harem
Beholden to the Throne

The Secrets of Xanos

A Shameful Consequence
An Indecent Proposition

Visit the Author Profile page
at Harlequin.com for more titles.

PROLOGUE

'HEY, *SHISHKA*.'

Daniil Zverev stiffened as he walked into the dormitory and heard what his friend Sev had just called him.

It would seem that *shishka* was now his new name.

Russian slang could hit just where it hurt, and tonight it did its job well.

Big gun.

Bigwig.

Big shot.

Daniil watched as Sev put down the book he had been reading.

'We were just talking about how you're going to go and live with the rich family in England, *shishka*.'

'Don't call me that again,' Daniil warned, and picked up the book and held it over his head. He made to rip the pages out but, as Sev swallowed, Daniil tossed it back on the bed.

He wouldn't have torn it—Sev only occasionally had a book to read—but Daniil hoped he would heed the warning.

'Did you find any matches?' Nikolai looked up from the wooden ship he was painstakingly building and

Daniil went into his pocket and took out the handful that he had collected when he had done his sweeping duty.

'Here.'

'Thanks, *shishka*.'

Daniil would do it; he would smash Nikolai's ship. His breathing was hard and angry as he stared down his friend.

The four boys were, in fact, far more than friends.

Yes, Daniil and Roman might be identical twins and Nikolai and Sev no relation, but all four had grown up together. With their dark hair and pale skin, they were the poorest stock amongst the poor. At the baby house they had stood in their cribs and called to each other at night.

Daniil and Roman had shared a crib.

Nikolai and Sevastyan had slept in their own on either side of the twins.

When they had graduated to beds they had been moved to the children's orphanage and placed in the same dormitory. Now, in the adolescent wing, they shared a four-bedroomed room.

Most considered them wild boys, troubled boys, but they were no real trouble to each other.

They were all they had.

'Touch my ship...' Nikolai threatened.

'Don't call me *shishka*, then. Anyway, there is no need to—I've decided that I'm not going to live in England.' Daniil looked over at Roman, his twin, who lay on his bed with his hands behind his head, staring at the ceiling. 'I'm going to say that I don't want to go. They can't make me.'

'Why would you do that?' Roman asked, and turned his head and fixed his brother with the cold grey stare that they shared.

'Because I don't need some rich family to help me. We're going to make it ourselves, Roman.'

'Yeah, right.'

'We are,' Daniil insisted. 'Sergio said…'

'What would he know? He's the maintenance man.'

'He was once a boxer, though.'

'So he says.'

'The Zverev twins!' Daniil was insistent. 'He says that we're going to make it…'

'Go and be with the rich family,' Roman said. 'We're not going to get rich and famous here. We're never going to get out of this hole.'

'But if we train hard we'll do well.' Daniil picked up the photo by Roman's bed. Sergio had brought his camera in one day a couple of years ago and had taken a photo of the twins and, because the others had nagged, he had then taken one of all four boys.

It was the photo of the two of them, though, that Daniil now held up as he spoke to his brother. 'You said that we would make it.'

'Well, I lied,' Roman said.

'Hey…' Sev had got back to reading but, even though he had just teased Daniil, he cared for him and could see where this was leading. 'Leave him, Roman. Let him make up his own mind.'

'No.' Roman sat up angrily. Things had been building for months, since they'd first been told about a family who wanted to give a good home to a twelve-year-old. 'He wants to blow off his one chance because he has this stupid dream that he can make it in the ring. Well, he can't.'

'We can,' Daniil said.

'*I* can,' Roman corrected. 'Or at least I could if I didn't have you dragging me down.' He took the picture of the two of them out of Daniil's hand and tossed it across the floor. There was no glass in the frame, but something broke then. Daniil felt something fracture somewhere deep inside.

'Come on,' Roman said. 'I'll show you who can really fight.'

He got up out of the bed and there was a buzz around the dormitory as the twins eyed each other.

Finally they would fight.

The Zverev twins trained all day.

Sergio put them through drill after drill and they pushed through all of them. The only complaint they ever had was that they wanted to spar. Sergio had refused to allow it until a few months ago, but even then it was always under Sergio's watchful eye. As an ex-boxer himself, he knew better than to start the boys too early.

These boys were beautifully built. Tall and long-limbed, they were fast, light on their feet and hungry.

He knew that with the right training the twins would go far.

What a package!

Two peas in a pod, two pitched minds and two angry youths.

All Sergio had to do for now was contain them.

But he wasn't there tonight.

'Tell the others,' Roman said, and the room started to fill, beds were pushed back to make floor space and the gathering spectators knelt on them.

'Show me what you've got,' Roman jeered, as he came out fighting. He had Daniil straight on the defensive, blocking punches and moving back.

No headgear, no gloves, no money to get them.

Not yet.

Roman gave him nothing, no rest, nowhere to hide, and Daniil, with everything to prove, fought back with all he had.

The other boys were cheering while trying not to, as they did not want to alert the workers.

Roman was at his fiercest, and though Daniil did his best to match him it was he who tired first. He moved in and took Roman in a clinch. He just needed a moment to rest but his brother shrugged him off.

Daniil went in again, holding on to his twin so that Roman couldn't punch him, doing his best to get back some breath before he commenced fighting again.

Roman broke the clinch and the fight restarted, both blocking punches, both taking the occasional hit, but then Daniil thought he was gaining ground. Daniil was fast and Roman rarely needed to rest but it was Roman who now came in for a clinch and leaned on his twin. Daniil could hear his brother's angry breathing but as he released him, instead of giving Daniil that necessary second to centre, Roman hooked him, landing an uppercut to Daniil's left cheek and flooring him.

Daniil came round to stunned faces. He had no idea how long he'd been knocked out but it had been long enough to have everyone worried.

Everyone except Roman.

'See,' Roman said. 'I do better without you, *shishka*.'

The staff had noticed that some of the dorms were empty and, alerted by the mounting cheers, had started running to the room where Daniil now lay, trying to focus.

Katya, the cook, took him into the warm kitchen, calling to her daughter, Anya, to bring the box of tape. Anya was in there, practising her dance steps. She was twelve and went to a dance school but for now was home for the holidays. Sometimes she would tease the twins and say that she was fitter than them.

Anya still had dreams and thought she would dance her way out of here.

Daniil had none now.

'Hey, what on earth were you doing?' Katya scolded. She gave Daniil some strong, sweet black tea and then she tried to patch up his face. 'The rich family don't want ugly...'

Daniil sat on a bed just a few days later, seemingly a million miles from home.

In the car he had looked at the small houses and shops as they'd passed them and when the car had turned a corner he had seen in the distance a large imposing red-brick residence. They had been driven down a long driveway and he'd stared at the lawns, fountains and statues outside the huge house.

Daniil hadn't wanted to get out of the car but he had, silently.

The door was opened by a man in a black suit who looked, to Daniil, to be dressed for a funeral or wedding but his smile was kind.

In the entrance Daniil stood as the adults spoke over him and then up the stairs he was led by the woman who had twice come to the orphanage and who was now his mother.

At the turn of the stairs there was a portrait of his new parents with their hands on the shoulders of a smiling dark-haired child.

He'd been told that they had no children.

The bedroom was large and there was only one bed, which looked out to vast countryside.

'Bath!'

He had no idea what she meant until she pointed to a room off the bedroom, and then she had gone.

Daniil had a bath and wrapped a towel around himself, just in time, because there was a knock at the door. It opened and she approached him with an anxious smile. She started to go through his things and kept calling him by the wrong name.

He wanted to correct her and tell her his name was pronounced *Dah-neel*, rather than the *Dae-ne-yuhl* she insisted on using, but then he remembered the translator explaining that he had a new name.

Daniel Thomas.

That woman, his mother, had rubber gloves on, and his clothes, his shoes were all being loaded into a large garbage bag that the man in the suit was holding. She was still talking in a language he didn't understand. She kept pointing to the window and then his cheek and making a gesture as if she was sewing and after several attempts he understood that she was going to take him to get his cheek repaired better than Katya had done.

He stared at the case as she disposed of his life and then he saw two pictures, which Daniil knew that he hadn't packed. Roman had slipped them in, he must have.

'*Nyet!*'

It was the first word he had spoken since they had left Russia and the woman let out a small worried cry as Daniil lunged for the photos and told her, no, she must not to get rid of them and neither could she touch them.

His mother had fled the room and the man in the suit

stood there for a while before finally coming to sit on the bed and join him in looking at the photos.

'You?' He had pointed to Daniil and then to one of the boys in the picture.

Daniil shook his head. 'Roman.'

The old man with kind eyes pointed to his own chest. 'Marcus.'

Daniil nodded and looked back at the photo.

Only then did Daniil start to understand that Roman didn't hate him; he had been trying to save him.

Daniil, though, hadn't wanted to be saved.

He had wanted to make his way with his brother.

Not alone, like this.

CHAPTER ONE

TECHNICALLY, LIBBY TENNENT LIED.

She had made it through the gold glass revolving doors and had walked across the impressive marble floor and was just at the elevators when a uniformed security guard halted her and asked where she was going. 'I have an appointment with Mr Zverev,' Libby said.

'Perhaps you do, but before you can take the elevator, first you have to sign in at Reception.'

'Oh, of course,' Libby responded airily, trying to look as if she had simply forgotten the procedure.

Everything about the place was imposing.

It was a luxurious Mayfair address and, even before the taxi had pulled up at the smart building, Libby had realised that getting in to see Daniil Zverev might not prove the cinch that her father had insisted it would be.

Libby walked over to the reception desk and repeated her story to a very good-looking receptionist, saying that she had an appointment to see Mr Zverev, silently hoping that the woman wouldn't notice that the appointment was, in fact, for her father, Lindsey Tennent.

'And your name?'

'Ms Tennent.' Libby watched as the receptionist typed

in the details and saw that her eyes narrowed just a fraction as she looked at the computer screen.

'One moment, please.'

She picked up the phone and relayed the information. 'I have a *Ms* Tennent here. She says that she has an appointment with Mr Zverev.' There was a moment's pause and then she looked at Libby. 'Your first name?'

'Libby,' she said, but then, realising that given the way the security was in this place she was likely to be asked for official ID, she amended, 'Short for Elizabeth.'

Libby tried to appear calm and avoided curling a stray strand of her blond hair around her finger or tapping her feet, as she did not want to appear nervous.

She *was* nervous, though. Well, not so much nervous, more uncomfortable that she had agreed to do this.

Maybe she wouldn't have to because the receptionist shook her head as she replaced the phone. 'Mr Zverev cannot see you.'

'Excuse me?' Libby blinked, not only at the refusal but that it came with no apology or explanation. 'What do you mean, I have—?'

'Mr Zverev only sees people by strict appointment and, Ms Tennent, you don't have one.'

'But I do.'

The receptionist shook her head. 'It is a Mr Lindsey Tennent who has a 6:00 p.m. appointment. If he was unable to make it then he should have called ahead to see if sending a replacement was suitable—Mr Zverev doesn't just see anyone.'

Libby knew when she was beaten. She had rather hoped they might not notice the discrepancy—as most places wouldn't. She was almost tempted to apologise for the confusion and leave, but her father had broken down in tears when he'd asked her to do this for him. Knowing just how much was riding on this meeting, she forced herself to stand her ground. She pulled herself as tall as her petite five-foot-three frame would allow and looked the receptionist squarely in the eye.

'My father was involved in an car accident earlier today, which is the reason that he couldn't make it, and sent me as a replacement. Now, can you please let Mr Zverev know that I'm here and ready to meet with him? He knows very well the reason for my visit, or perhaps you'd like me to clarify that here?'

The receptionist glanced at whoever was standing behind Libby and then to the left of her. Clearly Libby had a small audience. The receptionist must have decided that the foyer wasn't the place to discuss the great man's business because she gave a tight shrug.

'One moment.'

Another phone call was made, though out of Libby's earshot, and eventually the immaculate woman returned and gave Libby a visitor's pass. Finally she was permitted past the guarded barrier that existed around Daniil Zverev.

The elevator door was held open for her and she stepped in.

Even the elevator was luxurious. The carpet was thick beneath her feet. There was no piped music, just cool air and subdued lighting, which was very welcome on a hot summer evening after a mad dash across London to get here.

She should never have let her father talk into this, she thought.

In fact, she hadn't. When Libby had said yes to trying to persuade this man to come along to his parents' fortieth wedding anniversary celebration, it had been a Daniel Thomas she had expected to be meeting.

But just as she had been about to leave her father had called her back.

'Oh, there's something I forgot to tell you.'

Her father, who had been begging Libby to the point of tears, had then looked a touch uncomfortable and evasive. 'He goes under a different name now.'

'Sorry?' Libby had had no idea what he was talking about.

'Or rather it would seem that Daniel Thomas has recently reverted to his real name—Daniil Zverev. He was adopted.'

'Well, if he's gone back to his birth name, clearly there's a serious rift. I'm not going to interfere...'

'Libby, please,' her father begged. 'All Zverev has to do is show up and make a speech.'

A speech? The list of demands for Daniil had again increased. Show up, dance with aunts, be sociable, and now she had to ask him to make a speech!

No, Libby was not comfortable with this at all. She lived in her own dreamy bubble where the role of negotiator didn't exist. She was very forthright, in that she had an expressive face and a tendency to say what she was thinking. She also, to her parents' disquiet, had always refused to quietly toe the line.

'You never said anything about him having to make a speech.'

'Can you just talk to him for me, Libby? Please!'

Why the hell had she said yes?

Of course, she had looked Daniil up on her taxi ride here. Her father had said that face-to-face he was sure that Libby would be able to appeal to his conscience but it would seem, from her brief skim through several articles, that the esteemed financier previously known as Daniel Thomas didn't have one.

It was, one article observed, as if he saw everyone as the opposition and would step over whomever he had to if it meant he achieved his aim.

As for women—well, it would take far longer than a thirty-minute taxi ride to read up on that part of his history! The word *heartbreaker* was thrown around a lot. User. From what Libby could glean, his longest, for the want of a word, *relationship* had been a two-week affair with a German supermodel, who had been left devastated by their sudden ending.

Well, what did these women expect? Libby had thought when she'd read how some considered the break-up to have been cruel.

Why would anyone ever get involved with him?

Libby had never been one for one-night stands but it would seem Daniil Zverev was a master of them. She was cautious in relationships, never quite believing men who said that her dancing wouldn't get in the way and that they had no issue with the hours she devoted to her art.

Always she had been proved right to be cautious. Invariably the reasons for the break-ups were the same—that she was obsessed with ballet, self-absorbed and hardly ever free to go out.

Correct.

She'd told them the same at the start.

Libby got back from dwelling on her disastrous love life to trying to fathom Daniil.

Surprisingly, there had been little made of his name change—it was as if even the press was wary of broaching certain topics around him.

So, too, was Libby. She certainly didn't relish the prospect of asking him to play 'happy families.'

Of course, she felt like David going into face Goliath as she came out of the elevator and walked along a corridor, only to face another seriously beautiful woman who ran her eyes over Libby as she approached the desk.

'I'm here to see Mr Zverev,' Libby said, but her smile wasn't returned.

'Perhaps you would like to freshen up before you go through.'

'Oh, I'm fine, thank you.' Libby shook her head—she really just wanted to get this over and done with.

'You will find the ladies' room just down the hall and to your right.'

To her sudden embarrassment Libby realised that it was being suggested, and strongly so, that she *needed* to tidy herself up.

Could the great Daniil Zverev only lay eyes on perfect people? Was he only prepared to hold court with women at their coiffed best?

She held back the smart retort, though, and instead, blushing to her roots, took herself off to the ladies room. As she stepped inside and saw herself in a full-length mirror she was, though she would never admit it, rather grateful for the advice to take a little time before seeing Daniil.

It was a warm and windy August day and she had the hair to prove it.

Determined to keep practising and to maintain her skills, without the delicious routine of dance class and rehearsals, Libby had been home, warming up, when word had come in that her father had been involved in a car accident. Of course, she had just pulled on some leggings and a wrap over her leotard, grabbed her workbag and raced to the accident and emergency department.

Her head was still spinning with all her father had revealed that afternoon. The family business was in serious trouble and they needed this anniversary party to go ahead next month. For that to happen, though, Daniil's acceptance of his parents' invitation must be secured.

Libby couldn't think about her father's business troubles now.

She went through her huge bag and pulled out a fresh ivory wrap and put that on over her leotard and changed from leggings into a grey tube skirt. Her blonde hair was already tied back but messy so she brushed and retied it and pinned it up. Her face was devoid of make-up and she looked far younger than her twenty-five years. Somehow she didn't think fresh-faced would appeal to such a sophisticated man but Libby didn't have an awful lot in her make-up bag to work with. Some mascara made her blue eyes look bigger and she added some lip gloss too.

She'd just have to do.

Libby knew she didn't stand a hope with him. A man who had cut ties with his family so dramatically that he'd changed his name was hardly going to want to turn things around on her say-so.

And, anyway, Libby was the last person to tell someone else what they should do.

She, herself, didn't like free advice.

She'd be working in the family business if she did.

Resigned to being sent away even before she'd got out the first sentence almost took away the fear of meeting him.

Yes, she'd just say what she had to and then walk away. She would not allow herself to be intimidated.

Snooty Pants at Reception must have deemed Libby looked suitable now because she picked up the phone and informed him that his 6:00 p.m. appointment was here. 'However, as I said it is—' He must have interrupted her because she didn't finish explaining again that it was Libby rather than Lindsey who was there. 'I'll send her in.'

As Libby *finally* went to head for the door it would seem that she'd jumped the mark.

'You can leave your bag here.'

She was about to decline but again she realised it wasn't a suggestion so she put her bag down and headed for the door. As she was about to raise her arm she was halted.

'Don't knock, it irritates him. Just go straight through.'

Libby felt like knocking just for the hell of it!

And knocking again.

And then knocking again.

The thought made her smile.

Widely!

And that was how he first saw her.

Smiling at some secret joke, because, Daniil knew, nothing his PA would have said would have put her at ease.

She was a dancer.

He knew that not just from her attire but from her posture as she closed the door behind her, and she was fighting her dancer's gait as she walked a little way towards him and then paused.

As she stepped in Libby blinked. She was standing in a postcard view of London. She might just as well have bought a ticket for the London Eye, though there would never have been someone quite as delicious sitting opposite her there!

He had dark hair, dark eyes and pale skin and there was a livid scar across his left cheekbone. He sat straight in his seat at a very large desk, watching her with mild interest.

Despite the huge office, despite the vast space, he looked so formal and imposing that he owned every inch of it.

'Thank you for agreeing to see me, Mr Zverev,' she said, while privately, such was his impact, she rather wanted to turn and run.

'My, my, Mr Tennent,' Daniil said. 'What a high, clear voice you have.'

His own voice was deep and his words were dipped and richly coated in a chocolaty Russian accent, and as she realised he was alluding to the appointment being with her father her smile stretched further and she lost her fear.

'And, oh, Mr Tennent,' Daniil continued, his eyes taking in her slender bare legs, 'what smooth skin you have.'

She stood before him and, no, Libby wasn't scared in the least. Still she smiled.

'I think we both know, Mr Zverev...' she started, and then halted as she properly met those cold grey eyes that pierced her. She sent a silent apology to the women she had so merrily scorned for getting involved with him. She had never understood women who could simply leap into bed with a man but she had to wrestle to hold on to her conscience, for he was so beautiful, his stare so intense and so sexy that he could possibly have had her then.

She had to clear her throat so she could continue

speaking, and she had to recall their words just to find her thread.

Yes, that's right...

'I think we both know, Mr Zverev,' Libby said, 'that *you're* the big bad wolf!'

CHAPTER TWO

SURPRISINGLY, WHEN SHE was so bold as to call him the big bad wolf to his face, Daniil actually smiled. 'Indeed I am.'

Libby caught her breath. Those hooded, guarded features briefly relaxed, that deep red sulky mouth stretched and the cold grey eyes softened. Not a lot, just enough that, for a brief second, he didn't look quite so formidable.

But very quickly that changed and it was down to business.

'Take a seat,' he instructed.

Libby did, crossing her ankles and resting her hands in her lap.

'Would you like some refreshment?' he offered.

'No, thank you.'

'You're sure?' he checked.

'Quite sure.' Libby nodded, just as she realised she was terribly thirsty, yet she felt uncomfortable knowing what she was about to ask him and cross with her father for the position she was in.

Daniil reached across his desk and opened a bottle of sparkling water. It was chilled, she could see that from the condensation on the bottle, and, suddenly *very* thirsty, Libby heard the delicious fizzing sound as he opened it and then the lovely glug, glug, glug as he poured it into a heavy glass.

He didn't offer again.

Bastard.

But then he pushed the glass towards her, and with a slight roll of her eyes she took it. 'Thank you.'

He poured his own and she glanced at his hands—even they were beautiful, his fingers long and slender, his nails short and manicured.

'So?' Daniil said.

Oh, yes. She dragged her mind back to the reason she was there. 'My father is very sorry that he couldn't make it this evening. He was involved in a car accident earlier today.'

'I'm sorry to hear that,' Daniil said. 'He wasn't seriously injured, I hope?'

'Oh, no.' She was surprised at the concern in his voice. 'It's just a mild concussion…'

Daniil hid his smirk as her voice trailed off and he watched as Libby frowned. It was a very mild concussion. In fact, the doctor had come in just as Libby had been leaving and had told Lindsey that he could go home.

If this meeting with Daniil had been so pressing, so vital and urgent, then surely he could have made the effort and come?

'He needs to rest for the next forty-eight hours,' she said, though suddenly she felt as if she was convincing herself instead of him. 'As you know, he's an events planner and—'

'And the event that he is planning will not go ahead unless I attend.' Daniil broke into her chatter.

'Yes.' Libby took a sip of her water. 'Sir Richard is very adamant that without his son there…' She looked at

Daniil and saw the tiny rise of his eyebrows and she had the feeling he was laughing at her, though his lips did not move. 'Well, it's their fortieth wedding anniversary. That's quite an achievement these days.'

'What is?' Daniil checked.

'A forty-year marriage.'

'Why?'

Libby blinked at his question. 'Well, I guess if it's a happy marriage then it's quite an achievement.' She shot out a nervous laugh—he picked up on everything.

'I guess it is something.' Daniil shrugged. 'I have never made it past forty-eight hours...'

His eyes held hers, *really* held hers, and to her astonishment Libby realised that there was a warning there. A delicious warning perhaps, and Libby's own eyes narrowed at something she couldn't quite put her finger on.

One—she pondered, was he flirting with her?

Possibly, she conceded. A lot of work would have gone into honing his technique so he was just idly practising perhaps.

Two—if he could be so direct then so would she.

'There was that German supermodel...' Libby wagged her finger at him. 'You lasted two weeks with her, I believe.'

'You've done your homework,' Daniil said approvingly. 'Ah, yes, Herta. I followed her to a photo shoot in Brazil, not because I was lovesick, more that I had to check something...' His gorgeous index finger went to his Adam's apple.

'Sorry?'

'I kept thinking—she was so tall and that voice of hers was so deep...'

Oh, my God, he was shocking.

'And was she…?' Libby croaked.

'A she?' Daniil said, and nodded. 'She definitely was. Thank God.' He let out a low laugh and Libby forgot what planet she was on. It was Daniil who had to bring her back to earth. 'Go on,' he said.

She had two big guns to use on him and a very impatient target. She could almost sense her time with the great man was about to expire.

'Well, as you know, Lady Katherine is unwell,' Libby said. 'Extremely unwell.'

'Not so unwell that she can't throw a party,' Daniil pointed out.

'No, but…'

'But?'

She tried to trip or even make a tiny jiggle on his guilt switch but he just coolly stared back at her as she spoke. 'Well, there might not be a forty-first.'

'Is that it?' Daniil frowned.

'Sorry?'

'Your attempt to persuade me?'

She swallowed. She did think of her other big gun, that there was a letter awaiting him if he went and something about Sir Richard not giving Daniil's inheritance to his cousin, but, hell, Libby thought, how tacky was that, so she chose not to use it.

'That's it.' Libby sighed and gave in. 'I'm not very good at trying to persuade people. I tend not to bother, in fact.'

'Well, just so you know, your technique is all wrong,' he said. 'First, you should have given me all the shit, just laid it out on the table for me.'

'Such as?'

'You should have told me that I would have to go by

my adopted name if I attended—Daniel Thomas—and that I would be expected to give a speech…'

Libby sat with her mouth gaping, realising he was streets ahead of her.

'Then,' Daniil said, 'when you had my emphatic refusal, *then* you should have tried to persuade me and talk me round by pointing out my mother's declining health and such things.'

'Would it have worked?'

'Not on me,' he said. 'I'm just letting you know, for future reference, that you were working backwards with your technique because, had I dubiously agreed, there was still more you had to ask of me. You hit me too soon with the sob story.'

'Well, then, it's just as well this isn't my usual kind of work,' Libby said, and peered at him. He completely intrigued her. He was a stunning mix—arrogant and hostile yet somehow approachable.

'Tell your father the answer is no—I shall not be attending my parents' wedding anniversary celebrations.'

'Because?' she asked.

'I have no reason to, neither do I wish to share my decision-making process with you.'

'Was it always going to be a no?'

'Yes.'

'Then, why did you agree to see my father?'

'Well, he insisted that he had something to say that might change my mind. I notice that you didn't mention my inheritance going to Cousin George.'

'No.'

'Why not?'

'I have no reason to, neither do I wish to share my

decision-making process with you.' Libby parroted his words but he just smiled.

'You know you want to really.'

She did!

'Well—' Libby shuffled in her seat '—I happen to think that's blackmail.'

'That's my parents' favourite sport,' Daniil said. 'Anyway, I don't need a draughty old mansion on my hands. I loathe the place. I certainly have no wish to ever own it.'

Libby hated that she'd been talked into doing this, she really did. 'Look, I'm very sorry for interrupting you, Mr Zverev.'

'That's it?'

'Yes.' Libby beamed. 'I'll pass on your response to my father.'

'If he is annoyed at not getting his way, know that he would have lasted one minute with me. You can console yourself you did better than he ever could have.'

'Why?'

'I liked watching your mouth.'

'You can't say that.'

'Why not? You demanded to see me, you came into my office without a proper appointment, you don't get to dictate how I behave in here.'

He stood and she just about folded over in her seat as six feet two of heaven gracefully walked across the floor and retrieved his jacket from a stand. Well, he sort of flicked it off the hook and then slipped it on, all in one lithe motion.

'There's water,' Daniil said, 'and over there is a fridge with some nice contents. The bathroom is through there...'

'Sorry?'

'You're still sitting and I'm clearly on my way out so I assumed you were staying.'

'Oh!'

Even standing was a challenge with him in the room. Her legs had forgotten their role, and so had her head because she even bent down to retrieve her bag, which, of course, wasn't there.

'That's right, I left it at Reception.'

He made her seem slightly mad.

She felt slightly mad.

As she stepped out of his office it was like walking out of a ten-hour back-to-back session at the movies and blinking at the light.

Libby picked up her bag and gave Snooty Pants a smile then headed for the elevator but she jumped in quiet surprise when she realised that he was standing behind her.

'I thought that you'd have a special elevator,' Libby observed. 'One that only goes up.'

Yes, she thought, he would take her to heaven.

They stepped in and the doors closed and Libby waited for the most excruciating elevator ride of her life to commence, but instead it turned out to be the best ever.

He was checking his phone and then he looked up to where she stood. She was leaning against the wall, gazing at his stunning face, intrigued by his scar.

'Do you want an early dinner?' he said, and, just like that, he offered her a delectable slice of his time.

'Dinner?'

'Well, I'm hungry and I guess you didn't have time to eat in your haste to get to your critically injured father.'

Libby's lips twitched into a smile.

'And then,' Daniil continued, 'there would have been

all the shock and relief of finding out that he only had mild concussion.'

She laughed. 'No, I didn't have lunch.'

'So do you want dinner?' Daniil checked. 'But on one condition.'

They stepped out and walked across the foyer. She glanced at the receptionist who hadn't been going to let her in and Libby was tempted to poke out her tongue.

'What's the condition?' she asked.

'Know that I shan't be changing my mind.'

'About?' Libby frowned and then answered her own question—oh, yes, the reason she was there. 'I get that.'

They walked out and a car with a driver standing outside was waiting for him.

'How did he know you were on your way out?'

'Cindy would have rung down to alert him that I was leaving.'

Cindy!

Well, yes, she would be called that.

As she climbed into the car, one of the many things that Libby was thinking about was how much money she had on her and what the balance on her credit card was.

Her mother had always warned her to have enough money for a taxi ride home and she also wanted to know she had money enough on her card to pay for dinner.

He was, she had read, prone to walking off in the middle of a meal, or a holiday, or a photo shoot in Brazil. When bored, he did not push through politely.

He could leave at any moment, and she accepted that—this was transient and temporary.

She wouldn't have missed it for the world.

Now they were out of his vast office and in the smaller surroundings of a car, his size was more noticeable. Tall, his shoulders were wide, but as he had put on his jacket she had noted just how flat his stomach was.

She was small but he made her feel tiny as she sat beside him. 'Where are we going?'

'Somewhere nice,' he said.

Nice was a roped-off club that drew a crowd even on a Monday evening.

And it was very nice not to have to queue.

'Did you have a reservation?' Libby asked, as they were shown straight in and through.

'No, I never book anywhere,' he said as they took a seat. She put her bag on the floor and they put their phones down on the table. 'How can you know in the morning what you will want that night?'

Second warning bell.

She glanced around and people were staring at them.

She felt a little like she had when she'd done work experience at the library and the real worker had gone to lunch. Someone had asked her a question and had expected her to know the answer.

'I don't really work here,' Libby had wanted to say as she'd tapped away on the computer.

'I'm not really with him,' she wanted to correct the curious onlookers.

Except, to her absolute delight, tonight she was!

Oh, she knew it was a one-off, that she was here by default only, but it was such a lovely turn of events that she decided to simply enjoy it.

'What would you like to drink?' Daniil asked, as she read through the cocktail menu.

It was overwhelming.

Like him.

Just breathing normally was an impossible feat with him so near.

She gave a slightly helpless shake of her head, which was probably terribly unsophisticated but it was all she could manage.

'Champagne?' he checked, and she nodded, but when he gave the order and she heard just what champagne they would be drinking she knew she had better hold on to that attention span of his because her credit card would not be able to cover it.

The champagne was poured and the ice was truly broken when Libby's phone rang and Daniil glanced down and saw from Libby's caller ID that it was her father calling.

'Answer,' he said.

She did so.

'I'm sorry, Dad, I did speak to him but the answer's still no.'

Daniil watched her as she talked.

His invitation to take Libby to dinner had surprised him. She was nothing like his usual type, which was generally close to a foot taller and quite happy to sit bored and silent, just pleased to be seen out with him.

Libby Tennent didn't sit. She squirmed in the chair as she chatted, one hand was playing with her hair, her eyes were rolling and she was frantically blushing as she spoke with her father. 'No, I'd say that there's no chance of him changing his mind.'

Daniil watched.

'No, I wouldn't try calling him if I were you, Dad,' Libby responded when her father suggested he do just that. She gave Daniil a little wink. 'He's a very cold person.'

Daniil smiled and took a drink of his champagne.

'No, I think you're just going to have to accept that his answer is no. How are you feeling—?' she attempted, but he had already rung off.

She put down her phone and raised her palms in the air then looked up when Daniil started counting.

'One,' Daniil said, and Libby frowned. 'Two...' Just as she was about to ask what it meant, his phone rang. 'I still don't know how he got my private number.'

He took the call from Lindsey and was about to give his usual cold, brusque response, but, maybe because he knew that he'd be sleeping with his daughter in, say, an hour or so from now, Daniil was a touch more polite than he would usually be.

'Lindsey, I am sorry to hear about your accident. I'm blocking your number now. Don't try to get hold of me again.'

He rang off.

'I feel so bad for him,' Libby admitted. 'As well as cross with him for sending me to try to persuade you. I told him I didn't want to.'

'So why did you?'

Libby gave a tight shrug. 'He pointed out that, unlike June, my sister, I do nothing at all for the family business.'

'What does June do?'

'She's a chef.' Libby sighed. 'Who married a chef.'

'A very handy daughter to have for an events planner.'

Libby gave a glum nod. 'Unlike me.'

'What about your mother?'

'She works with my father.'

'Do you get on?'

'We do but...' Libby gave another tight shrug. 'I'm far too demonstrative for the lot of them. You know, sometimes I'm sure that I'm adop…' She swallowed down the most appalling faux pas but Daniil just gave a wry smile.

'At least I knew that I was.'

'I'm sorry.' Libby winced. 'That was thoughtless.'

'What is it with the English and guilt?' he asked. 'It doesn't bother me a bit, and there's no reason for guilt about your father—it's not your fault his business is about to go under.'

Libby shot him a look.

'How?' she asked. How did he know?

'Does he usually chase up every non-attendee with such vigour?'

'No.'

'Clearly this party is very important to him.'

'It is.'

'Guilt and manipulation are terrible bedfellows,' Daniil said. 'My parents must know that your father is desperate, so they used him to get to me. In turn, he knows that he's getting nowhere, so he guilts you into coming to see me, hoping I would not be able to say no to your lovely blue eyes.' He wagged his finger at her. 'Tut-tut, Libby.' Then he gave her a thin smile. 'So are you close to your parents?'

'For the most part,' Libby said. 'I think all families have their issues that drive each other crazy but if you love…' She hesitated as she remembered that Daniil was estranged from his parents. 'Do you care about them at all?'

'No.' He shook his head but offered no elaboration.

'Were you ever close to them?'

'I never let myself get close to anyone.'

She frowned, but said nothing at first. It wasn't for her to correct him, it wasn't for her to say he was wrong. She had stepped into his world uninvited and she didn't make his rules or get to tell him how he should be.

'Why?' Libby asked, and from the blush spreading on her neck both knew she wasn't just discussing his lack of relationship with his parents.

'Because it leads to expectations that it might last and, in my opinion, nothing lasts. Libby...' Daniil was incredibly direct. 'You do understand that whatever happens tonight won't change my mind about attending my parents' party?'

'Yes.'

He didn't believe her for a moment. 'You're sure?' he checked.

She nodded.

'Because,' he warned, 'that would be very foolish of you.'

'I know,' she said, 'and I hope that you understand that your expensive champagne won't buy a night in bed with me.'

'Yes.'

'You're sure?'

'Yes.' Daniil nodded. 'But my charm might.'

Libby laughed.

He was bad but it felt so good.

'What about you?' he asked. 'You know about my two-week record, what's your record in a relationship?'

Libby thought for a moment. 'Eighteen months,' she said. 'Though the last six don't really count.'

'Why?'

'We were seriously limping along by then.' She thought back to that time—the constant knot in her stomach at the juggling of too many balls. It had been a relief when the relationship ball had finally fallen and she could fully immerse herself in dance. 'Apparently I was too focused on my career.'

'Instead of him?' Daniil checked, and Libby nodded. 'That's his issue.'

'Perhaps,' she sighed. 'I keep telling myself that.'

'Then, it's time to start believing it.'

The waiter came and Libby ordered the French onion soup as her main and Daniil asked for two steaks and a green salad.

When they were alone she looked back at him. 'Two?'

'I have a big appetite,' he said, and then admitted that he was curious about her order. 'I'm surprised that you didn't ask for them to leave off the cheese and bread. Isn't that what most ballet dancers do?'

'Ha.' Libby gave a wry smile. 'Unfortunately the only time I'm not hungry is when I'm anxious or stressed. The moment I'm happy I'm constantly starving. How did you know I was a dancer?'

'You were trying very hard to keep your legs parallel and not walk like a duck when you came into my office.'

Oh. Her thighs were definitely parallel now—in fact, they were squeezed tightly together just from the delicious brush of his knees.

'Professional?' Daniil asked.

'Ex.' For the first time he saw that happy smile waver. 'Well, I guess I shall be again soon but in a different way—I'm looking at two rentals tomorrow so that I can start my own dance school. You know the saying, those that can't, teach.'

'That doesn't sound like something you would say to somebody else,' Daniil observed.

'No,' Libby admitted.

'So why do you say it about yourself?'

'I'm guess I'm not where I'd hoped to be.'

'Which is?'

For the first time conversation faltered.

Libby took a large slug of champagne before speaking. 'My biggest part never happened...' She saw his small frown. 'I was understudy once. You know when they say, "Break a leg"? Well, I meant it. But, of course, she didn't.'

'You never meant it.'

'No,' she admitted. 'I'd have loved her to get at least one migraine, though.'

Daniil smiled and now so did she.

'Look, I've accepted that the small roles I get aren't going to lead to anything bigger. I love ballet, seriously I do, but it's not *everything*. It's almost everything but if you want to go far then that's what it has to be. I've also had a couple of injuries that I haven't come back from...'

'Such as?'

'You never want to see my feet,' she said.

'Oh, but I do.'

Said feet's toes were curling at another press of his knee, so much so she was almost tempted to flick off her shoe and place it in his lap.

Help!

'Anyway, the last fracture I had demanded rest and you just can't. You have to push through but I realised that I can't keep doing it any more. I know I'm not going to go far, at least not anywhere that's going to pay more than my rent, so I've been studying to teach. I'm actually excited about it now. I've had my depression.'

'You thought that your life was over?'

'Oh, yes,' she readily agreed, because for months she had not been able to imagine leaving her dream behind, but now, well, she was happy with what she'd achieved and excited for all that was to come.

Almost.

There was an ache there—that she would never be a part of a big production again, never audition—but she avoided touching it for now.

'And so tomorrow you look at places to open your own dance school?'

'I do.'

'Good luck, then.' He raised his glass and they chinked them.

The soup was sublime, the crust perfect, and she poked a hole to get to the lovely brown broth beneath.

'Tell me about the places you are looking at tomorrow,' he said.

'Well, there's one not very far from where you work and it has the rent to prove it. Then there's one in the East End, which I can afford and it already has mirrors...'

'So it was once a dance studio?'

'Yes.'

'Why did it close down?'

Her spoon paused midway to her mouth. 'Don't spoil my appetite.'

'No, these are the questions that you need to ask. Trust me, I know these things.'

She gave him a tight smile. 'I don't think teeny-tiny dance studios are your area of expertise...'

'Business is business.'

'Perhaps, but it's very personal to me.'

'There's nothing wrong with being personal,' he said. His knees did not dust hers now, they were there touching hers and pressing in a little and, yes, they were officially flirting, and if he could be nosey then so could she. 'How did you get your scar?'

He gave a tiny shake of his head as a response.

Just that.

No evasiveness, no excuses, just a tiny shake of his head that told her not to go there.

It intrigued her, though.

The scar was jagged and raised and, given his billions, Libby wondered why he didn't get it tidied up.

His teeth were beautifully capped—well, she assumed that they were because no genes were *that* good—and clearly, from everything else she could see, from his immaculate hair to his exquisitely cut suit, Daniil took care of his appearance.

Apart from that scar.

They chatted, or rather she did. He was extraordinarily good at getting information out of her. Where she lived, where she'd gone to school, where she'd danced.

And as he went to top up her glass and only a trickle came out, she realised most of the conversation had been about her.

'I'll get more,' he said, about to call for a waiter, but Libby stopped him.

'Not for me—I'd pass out.'

'Dessert?'

He saw the wrestling in those lovely blue eyes. Libby knew their time was up, yet she simply couldn't walk away.

'Please.'

The menus came again and she looked through her choices, tempted to order the chocolate soufflé, just to prolong the inevitable end.

'Crême brulée,' Libby settled for instead. 'You?'

'Just coffee.'

It was eight twenty-seven when her dessert was served and it was already over.

'Nice?' Daniil asked.

'Very.' Libby nodded, yet she could more than sense his distraction. He glanced out to the street and once more she saw him check the time.

Thank him for dinner and go home, Libby told herself, but instead she dragged things out a tiny bit by going to the loo. Then she had a coffee and little chocolate mints but all too soon their drinks were done and all that was left for Libby to do was slip a serviette into her bag as a memento of the evening.

A few moments later they walked out into the street and there, waiting for him, was his driver.

'I'm going to get a taxi home,' Libby said.

'Why would you do that when I have a car waiting?'

A car that, from the way she was feeling, would only lead to his door. She looked up at him. 'I think we both know why.'

'Well,' he said, 'it was very refreshing to meet you, Ms Tennent.'

'It was very daunting to meet you.' Libby smiled. 'Well, it was at first.'

'And how about now?'

His hands went to her hips, the move sexy and suggestive as he framed where their minds were. Libby had a sudden urge to be lifted by him, to wrap her legs around him.

'I'm very daunted,' she admitted, 'though the middle bit was fun.'

It *was* daunting only because she was about to be kissed by the devil.

Why the hell did I order French onion soup, she thought, wondering if she could press Pause on him and scrabble in her bag for mints.

Oh, that was right, she'd had those chocolate ones with her coffee.

'What are you thinking?' Daniil said, because her eyes were darting and it was as if she was having a conversation with herself.

'I'm not going to tell you.'

He didn't test the waters, he didn't start slowly, he just lowered his head from a great distance and Libby got the most thorough kissing of her life. His lips parted hers, his lips, not his tongue, and he held her so firmly that even as she went to rise onto her toes still he held her down. And when her lips were opened his tongue tipped hers and he explored her, not particularly softly. His jaw was rough and delicious, and when she tried to kiss him back she was met by a refusal.

This was his kiss to her, his mouth said. It wasn't a dance of their mouths. He didn't even lead, he simply took over, tasting her, stilling her, making her body roar into flame with his mouth. So solid was he Libby felt as if she were leaning against a wall. Even when someone knocked into them they were barely interrupted, such was the shield of him.

His kiss had her hot, right there in the street, but the only movement he allowed was to let her hands reach for his chest. She slid her fingers over the cool fabric of his shirt and found the nub of his nipples. Yes, she was hot and aching for more, her hips were pushing frantically against his hands so their bodies might have more contact. But then, when he coiled her so tight, he released her mouth. He'd let her glimpse a fraction of what being held by him felt like and then he cruelly removed the pleasure.

She sucked in the summer night air while craving his mouth again.

'Bed,' Daniil said.

'I don't…' Libby halted. What had she been about to say—that she didn't want to?

Well, yes, she did.

Since the age of eight, dancing had come first, which had meant self-discipline.

In everything.

How nice to stand here on the brink of making a decision based purely on now, on her own needs and wants right at this moment.

And she did want.

So she chose to say yes when the wisest choice might have been to decline.

'Bed.' Libby nodded and then blinked at her response. She didn't retract it but her voice was rueful when she spoke next. 'I am so going to regret this in the morning,'

'Only if you expect me to love you by then.'

Third warning bell.

She could turn and walk away now.

'Oh, no,' Libby said, and in that at least she was wise. 'Then, there's no reason for regret.'

CHAPTER THREE

THE SECURITY TO get past for his penthouse apartment ri-valled that at Daniil's office.

First his driver spoke into an intercom and gates opened that led to an underground car park. From there they walked to another elevator that was only opened when Daniil typed in a code and gave his name in his low sexy drawl.

Up into a foyer they went, where they were greeted, and then it was another elevator up to his place.

Once inside, he threw his jacket over a couch and poured them both a drink and then sat on one of the large sofas, leaving Libby standing for a moment, taking it all in.

Daniil was very used to having women in his home. He didn't like going to theirs. Here, he was in control.

What he wasn't used to, though, was a woman like Libby. Her flat shoes made no sound on his marble tiles as she went over and looked out at the view and, Daniil was sure, she had another conversation going on in her head.

He lived above the clouds, Libby thought, or at least that was how it felt. They were so high up that she could be flying now, or in a hot-air balloon.

'You don't sound like a pony clipping around,' he observed.

'Ah, yes, noise irritates you.' Libby smiled as she nursed a brandy and stared out at a dusky London, the sky flaring orange and promising that tomorrow would be another hot day, and she thought about the lead-up to tonight. 'I was going to knock on your office door just to annoy you. And then knock again.'

'Is that why you were smiling when you came in?' Daniil asked, as he recalled thinking that she had been laughing at some private joke.

Now she shared it.

'It was.' Libby turned from one delicious view to another.

Him.

'Do you know that I was sent off to clean myself up before Cindy would let me in to see you?'

'Of course.'

'I felt like I was at school and they were doing uniform inspection,' she said, and then got back to peering at Big Ben and wondering if you could hear the chimes from in here, but her question never got asked because he spoke first.

'Do you have your navy panties on?'

She wanted to lift her skirt and flash her bottom at him and she laughed out loud as she imagined doing so. 'I'm most unlike me tonight,' she admitted.

'In what way?'

She thought for a long moment, wondering how best to describe the sheer heady pleasure of self-indulgence, how, till today, she had contained herself, unless she was dancing. Instead of saying so, though, she shook her head, just as Daniil did when there was something he would rather not discuss.

He accepted her silence.

'I'm most unlike me, too,' he said.

Usually he'd be just about on his way out.

Dinner with Libby had been very civil and certainly it was early to be home. More pointedly perhaps, they hadn't kissed their way up in the lift, neither were they in bed already.

Instead, she wandered around and, rarely at ease with that, he let her.

It was a vast floor space; the walls, to the sides of the glass one, were brick, and the effect was amazing against the night sky. There was a storm rolling in and it was a sight to behold, the sky lighting up pink in the distance with each strike, yet there were no rumbles of thunder to be heard; rather she felt them. Looking out, it was almost as if you were on a very high balcony, suspended there on the outside. In fact, it was a little dizzying, as if you should be able to feel the breeze. After a few moments of taking it in, Libby stepped back and, as she did so, she felt she should be closing doors behind her. 'Your home is stunning.'

It was.

The dark leather sofas were so wide and inviting she could happily sleep on a quarter of one of them, and naturally there were all the mod cons.

Except there was something missing.

There was no artwork on the walls, no photos on the shelves.

'No books!' Libby exclaimed.

'I read online.'

'But what about all your old ones?'

'I dispose of them when I'm done.' Daniil shrugged as Libby almost fainted in horror at the thought of him callously tossing them out.

Well, there's your lesson, she warned herself. She'd be shivering in the recycle pile tomorrow, with all evidence of her ever being here tidied away by his maid.

Yes, it was somehow, despite the beauty, sterile.

The kitchen was something that would have any serious cook weeping with envy but, unlike her sister, Libby wasn't a cook by any stretch of the imagination so she passed by quickly.

'You don't like the kitchen?' he called over his shoulder as she walked past it.

'It's a kitchen,' she said.

She hesitated as she approached the master bedroom, where she would be performing later, but was surprised at her lack of stage fright.

They might not even make it to the bedroom, Libby sighed, because right now she was fighting the temptation to turn around and run over and do him on the sofa.

She could feel his eyes on her and she had a prickly, excited feeling that at any moment he might choose to pounce.

What a bedroom, she thought as she peered in.

Just a bed.

That was it.

There was one perfect, vast, four-poster bed, which was dressed in white and was up against a huge brick wall.

No art on the walls, no mirrors...

It was curiously beautiful in its simplicity because there was nothing and nowhere to hide.

'Where do you put your clothes?' she called from the doorway.

'There is dressing room behind the wall to your right.'

There were no bedside tables, either.

'Where do you put your glass of water?'

'I get up if I want a drink.'

'Condoms?'

'Ha!' He laughed at her brevity. 'I have a woman who hands one over at the necessary moment...'

She turned and rolled her eyes.

'Under the pillow,' he said.

'Oh.' Libby felt curiously deflated. 'I thought you'd at least have a button to push or something for that.'

Again, it was very sterile, almost clinical, but terribly, terribly sexy too. She was incredibly turned on and almost ached for him to come over but still he sat, quietly watching her.

She let out a breath and chose not to enter the bedroom for further inspection; instead, she wandered some more.

There was a large, very neat study; again, though, there were no books, no photos and no clutter.

It was all so beautiful and yet so empty.

She came to another door and went to open it.

'Libby.'

She turned and he gave a slight shake of his head, the same one he'd given when she'd asked about his scar.

No excuse, no explanation, just a warning as to what was out of bounds.

Now he stood and moved in that same lithe way he had in the office and she felt suddenly nervous as he took off his tie.

It was a delicious nervousness that started between

her legs and worked up to her stomach and then caused
a blush to spread on her neck.

'Come on,' he said, and walked towards the bedroom.

No kiss, no 'whoops, how did we end up here,' no
words of endearment even.

This was sex, possibly at its most basic. Really, she
should hot tail it out of there, Libby knew, and yet his lack
of affection, his cold instructions turned her on rather
than off. She had never felt so drawn to anybody. The
ease and unease she felt with Daniil was a heady com-
bination. She would possibly have followed him to the
moon right now and so she chose not to refuse this rare
invitation.

'Can anyone see in?' she asked, looking out of the vast
windows and noting the lack of drapes or blinds.

'No.'

'You're sure?'

'Quite sure,' Daniil said, and gestured for her to come
to the window, where she had the same giddy sensation
of stepping outside. 'See there…' He pointed to the left
and she saw the soft glow behind a large window. He told
her it was the home of a rather promiscuous junior royal
and above that lived a film star. 'Like an ambulance,'
Daniil said, 'you can see out but not in.'

'Have you ever been in an ambulance?' she asked.

'A few times.'

She turned and looked at his cheek, wondering if now
she'd find out how he'd got that scar. 'For?' she fished.

'For…' Daniil said, and moved his mouth to her ear as
if to reveal a secret. Libby stood there, tense in anticipation, but no words were uttered. There was just the soft
sensation of his lips on her lobe, a decadent hush as his
mouth worked its way down her neck, her skin alive to

his touch but her mind sparking in frustration at his refusal to connect with her.

She jerked back and he raised his head and saw the glitter of frustration in her eyes.

'You don't need my life story, Libby.'

She wanted it, though.

She walked off towards the bed and sat there, her legs dangling over the edge as she tried to pull herself out of a sulk.

One night, she reminded herself, but already she was in over her head—how could one night ever be enough of this man?

She watched as he removed his shirt, and when he took it off she felt her jaw clench.

She knew bodies; it was her job to after all.

His was seriously beautiful—his abdomen, which she had already gauged as flat was toned and taut, his chest was so powerful and defined she was reminded of a huge butterfly spreading its wings. His arms were muscled, though long and slim, but she frowned at the dark bruise on his rib cage. She was about to ask what had happened but then saved herself from another rebuff and delivered an instruction instead.

'Turn around,' she said, and blinked at herself, finding it a little odd that she'd dared to ask, but there was a thrill when he obliged.

His back was like art; she could see the muscles beneath the white skin, and her colleagues would have fainted in pleasure just to see this.

She watched as he removed the rest of his clothing and then when he turned and she saw him naked she didn't pretend not to look, she just stared at his growing erection, as dangerous and as beautiful as him, ris-

ing from straight black pubic hair, and for tonight this
pleasure was hers.

'Get undressed,' he said, and he took her hand and
pulled her to a stand, but instead of leaving her there he
held her and her exposed skin was on fire against him.
She pressed her cheek against his chest and, as direct as
he was, she inhaled him, feeling him under her hands.
She ran her hands over his hips and to his buttocks and
she wanted her fingers on his spine.

Later.

Her eyes still glittered, but now it was with the pleasure to come, and when he released her she started to
undo her ivory wrap.

'Wait.'

He went and lay on the bed and stretched out that long
body and then nodded for her to continue.

She had a little trouble with the knot, only because she
was watching him and feeling his eyes carefully take in
any flesh she exposed. She was too small to worry with a
bra but her breasts felt heavy and her nipples were swollen and jutting out of her pale leotard.

She went to take down her skirt.

'Slowly,' Daniil said, and then he gave the same instruction she had. 'Turn around.'

Libby obliged.

First she kicked off her shoes and then rolled the skirt
down over her hips, bent and took off her skirt, and heard
his low moan of approval and knew he was stroking
himself.

She stood and lowered one strap of her leotard and
fought not to turn around.

She lowered the other one and slid it down past her
shaking thighs and then bent to take the leotard over her

feet. Without instruction, she held that position a little longer than necessary before coming back to a stand.

'Turn around.'

Naked, she stood and she loved the examination of his eyes, over her tiny bust, down her stomach and to her small blond mound.

Yes, she hadn't waxed in a while but, thank God, she'd shaved her legs that morning. Then she stood, legs a little crossed and one ugly foot on top of the other as his eyes went there.

'I love your feet,' he said. 'You know pain.'

'Is that what you're into?' Libby swallowed.

'No,' he said. 'I'm just saying I like it that you persisted. Don't be embarrassed by them.'

'Phew.'

'Worried I was going to spank you?'

'No.'

Technically, Libby Tennent lied.

In truth, he could put her over his knee this minute and she'd be delighted, and *that* worried her because she'd never thought like that in her life.

Yes, she was most unlike herself tonight.

And yet, when he called her over, when he said, 'Come here,' she was more herself than she had ever allowed herself to be, for she did as she wanted and went easily to him.

She climbed onto the bed but now she did not await instruction or summons. She knelt over him and kissed him, and he went to move his head but, no, she persisted, for it was her turn to kiss him now.

His lips were relaxed and accepting and she caressed them with hers, slipping in her tongue between them to get the lovely soft taste as his fingers took care of the ache in her breasts.

Usually Daniil did not care to linger, but tonight he dared to.

It was a night of firsts for both of them—for Libby it was a night of pure self-indulgence, for Daniil a brief break from resistance. Tonight he let himself feel—the softness of her lips and the breath that was sweet, the moans of her pleasure just from his taste and the soft shape of her breast that warmed and swelled to his palm.

Yes, it was a night of indulgence. Her lips never left his as she moved over him, sat naked on his stomach and kissed him more deeply. His hands left her breasts and slid down her waist but their ache was soon sated as he moved her higher and, pulling her down, took one breast in his mouth.

She pushed up on her knees, leaned forwards and gave him the full taste of her breast and the freedom to let his hands roam over her buttocks.

She felt incredible to Daniil—no silicone, no wobbly bits, just hard muscle beneath his fingers—and he pressed in as his mouth sucked harder.

She wanted more of the press of his fingers and the suction of his mouth, then he eased into her cold, long fingers, and she had a heady memory of his beautiful fingers caressing a glass and they were now inside her.

'Cold hands,' Libby breathed.

'Cold heart,' Daniil mumbled, with a mouthful of breast.

'I don't care…'

Her face was a furnace, her moans were ones of reproach as she berated herself for being so easy, so loose, and it had nothing to do with their fleeting time together, more that she was fighting not to come.

Daniil loved a fight; he stroked her so deeply, he got right up and into her oiled, heated space till she gripped tight on his fingers, and still he did not relent, stroking her down till she knelt on him breathless.

'I'd be a terrible male,' Libby said. 'It would all be over…'

'You'd be snoring,' he said, looking up at her shuttered eyes. 'And I'd be lying all tense and frustrated.'

He laughed at his own joke and lay with his fingers inside her, laughing when usually sex was a serious pursuit for him.

And then, because this night was more pleasurable than expected, he rested on the ropes and planned the next round, for he would take her to the limit; he would enjoy the lithe body that came so easily to his hand.

He lifted her so she sat high on his chest, her legs astride him, but he moved them so that her legs were over his shoulder and then he sat up.

'What…?'

Her eyes snapped open as she was lifted up.

God, he was strong.

His hands held her hips, and when she was sure she would topple he secured her with his mouth, burying his face in her sex.

Her legs were over his shoulders and down his back, and it took a moment to balance, but when she did, oh, my. He just held her and sucked her and there was nothing to hold on to, just mid-air and his hands on her hips and the bliss of his mouth. He moved her as he wanted, he tasted her absolutely, he drew from her words that she'd never uttered with each probe of his tongue.

'Never stop,' Libby begged as she came, loving the way he pushed her to the limit.

He had to stop, or he'd be coming to mid-air.

Daniil loved sex, for his own pleasure, but feeling her flicker to his tongue, that musky scent had him giddy and right on the edge himself.

He dropped her.

And she loved that he did.

The slam of the mattress on her back, the slight disorientation as she tried to locate the pillows, just to sheath him, but she was upside down in his bed.

'I'd better warn you…' He didn't need to. She saw he was more than ready as he slipped the condom on and he could come now and he'd still be her best lover.

His lips were shiny from her as he came over her and kissed her, and had she had any manners she'd have parted her legs, but she loved the roughness of his hairy thigh as he dealt with that.

She lay, a lazy, drunk-on-lust lover, hazy and giddy from two orgasms and trying to find brief pause, but there was none. There was a shrill of nervousness in her as she looked into ice and then surly lips spread into a ghost of a smile and she knew that she was about to find out what it was to be taken.

'Oh…' Libby said, as she was rapidly stretched, and she looked up into those cold grey eyes that were open to hers and she didn't need kissing, she just drowned in his pleasure and chose to enhance it—her arms raised as she gripped the wooden slats at the foot of the bed.

Rough were the hands that pulled her down but she held on firmly.

'Libby,' he said, and tugged her down again but she

did not let go, holding on as he took her, shackled by their thoughts, and it was a decadent bliss.

Oh, one night was not enough. It was her only tangible thought as he swelled within her, but still he did not give in.

'Come...' she begged, because she would at any moment. The noise alone signalled the end, he was so fast and so pumped, but still he would not unleash. He slowed and she clenched around his thick tip, gripped and released and watched his lips part as she played him at his own game, a game where both won, for he drove fully into her then, a punishment for daring to goad him, a delicious internal wrestle to take the lead.

Beneath him, she still came out on top, for Libby arched into him, pressed her hands into his buttocks, urged him and fully partook, but then, as her legs went to wrap around him, as she went to cling to him and share in the journey home, he took the lead.

His legs came to the sides of hers, halting their progress to his hips. Still he thrust as he trapped her thighs in his.

She went to protest, but his mouth smothered hers.

She lay there immobile and let out a sob as his pelvis opened and aligned fully with hers, his length sliding in so deep, the friction of him so relentless she lay there pinned, trying to remember to breathe, then deciding she didn't even need to because she was floating and sinking at the same time as he said something, presumably in Russian, presumably very bad, and he unloaded within her.

'Oh...' It was all she could manage.

It was an orgasm so deep that she cried.

Real tears.

And Libby, during a very difficult year, had refused to cry.

Best of all, he didn't comfort her afterwards.

He simply let her be.

It was exceptional bliss.

CHAPTER FOUR

'*NYET.*'

Daniil was half-asleep when her fingers set to work on his back.

'Shut up,' Libby said. She had promised herself a little dalliance with that back. 'It's my one-night stand, too.'

He frowned at her words for usually women were only too eager to please him and yet she made it sound as if she was pleasing herself.

Libby was.

As he rolled onto his stomach she climbed on and sat on his lower back and found herself in heaven.

His back was truly beautiful and his shoulders were just so wide that she could work for hours and never unravel all the knots, but feeling some of them dissolve beneath her fingers she carried on.

'What was that?' he asked as one minute in he realised it wasn't some sensual massage he was getting but a deep-tissue one. Right into his deltoid her slender fingers burrowed.

'You'll be in agony the day after tomorrow,' Libby promised. 'And the next day, but maybe by Friday you'll remember me fondly.'

Daniil did not like massage but her hands were so precise and expert that he let himself sink into it.

They were both in bliss.

Libby loved feeling his neck loosen and how he moaned with the pleasure of pain at times as she located a tense area. Down she slid and went to his buttocks and sustaining the pressure with her thumb did a muscle-stripping technique and he let out a small curse but did not tell her to stop.

In fact, he spoke, trusting her enough to let her get on as he asked her the question she hadn't answered.

'Why are you most unlike yourself tonight?'

Her hands paused for a moment and she found she was frowning as she worked out her answer. 'Maybe I'm just working out who I am without...'

Libby didn't finish. She didn't need to; they both knew she had been consumed by the dancing world for a very long time. She pressed her palms into Daniil's loins, lifting up a little so that more of her weight was on him, and shifted the conversation away from herself. 'So why are *you* most unlike yourself tonight?'

Daniil gave a low laugh that she felt in her hands before he answered, 'Because I'm still awake.'

She gave him a light slap between his right buttock and thigh for his response but she laughed, too, and they both paused a moment. She felt him shift a little to get comfortable, felt the resurgence of desire, but it wasn't sex that drew her closer to him in that moment—it was the shared moment of laughter and being herself.

Her most honest self.

She turned her head and looked out of the window and never again would she look at even a photo of Big Ben without remembering her time with him.

Today was supposed to have been the hardest day.

She had been warming up, at home alone, when her father had rung.

It had been her first day without dance class and now, when all the white noise had gone, everything she'd told her family, her flatmate, her colleagues, her friends, *herself* even, hushed. There, twenty minutes before the close of the day, she watched the storm over London and thick drops of water sliding down the windows, and she told him the *real* reason behind leaving the dance company she had loved.

'I jumped before I was pushed.' Libby voiced her truth. 'I wasn't even getting the small roles anymore.'

He didn't turn and kiss her, he didn't dim the pain with sex, he just let her fingers work his back. 'At least you jumped,' Daniil said. 'Most people have to be prised kicking and screaming from something they don't want to let go of.'

'That was almost me—I took forever to read the writing on the wall,' she admitted. 'I should have gone six months, maybe a year ago but I clung on to the bitter end. I'm crap at dignified exits—I can't even end a text conversation gracefully, let alone my career.'

'It must have been hard to let it go.'

And let it go she finally had, yet it hurt so much to have done so.

He heard her sniff and tears came again and he felt the drops of her tears on his skin. He let her cry awhile before speaking on.

'So now you fly solo,' Daniil said.

'I don't want to, though.'

'No choice sometimes.'

She liked it that he didn't fob her off, that he didn't tell

her, as others repeatedly had, that as one door closed...
when the simple fact was that she'd loved being on that
side of the door. Neither did he tell her how the greatest
opportunities were often born from the darkest times...
Being a part of a dance company had been a lifelong
dream and it was an opportunity that was now gone.

She carried on with his back and then there was silence, a lovely silence that Daniil usually only achieved
when he was here on his own. And it was better than
being alone because he really wasn't thinking about
where he was. Instead, he was thinking of where he'd
come from, which was a place in his mind he rarely vis-
ited from the vantage point of calm.

He'd never wanted to leave the orphanage. It had almost killed him to be prised from his friends and his twin
and thrust into a world that he hadn't wanted to inhabit,
and then she spoke again.

'I wanted to work with what I had,' she said.

In that moment he understood her and she understood
him; in that moment they were both pushed reluctantly
through the same portal of change and he remembered
his resistance. Daniil recalled with clarity how he had
wanted to be back with his brother and friends and a
world he had been told he should be happy to have left.
He thought of Sergio and how they'd raced from school
to the makeshift gym. Of Katya and strong, sweet tea
and a kitchen that had been big and always warm. Of
nights spent talking into the darkness and how the four
of them would speak with certainty about the world they
were going to change.

Instead, he'd had to learn to somehow coexist with a
family he could never be a part of, a headmaster who had

done all he could to quash rebellion and a cousin who had goaded and bullied him.

He, too, had had to make his way in a place he would have preferred not to be.

Libby knew there was nothing he could say that might make this better and was certain that he could never understand but then, as he spoke, she realised he did.

'Being resourceful sucks.' His response was sleepy but it hit the mark and Libby smiled unseen.

'It truly does.'

She worked his neck till it was pliant and then ran her hands down a very loose spine and then, tired now, bent and gave his shoulder a kiss and moved off him to lie down, liking the feel of his arm over her chest as he pulled her a little bit closer.

Neither moved all night.

In fact, Libby woke up exactly as she'd fallen asleep, on her back with his arm across her chest, and she turned to steal a look at him.

He was starting to wake up and he needed a razor and she'd never woken to such male beauty before.

Regret?

God, no.

Her whole body felt…well, it felt as if she'd been in for a tune-up.

He woke to her stretch and smile.

'Bad girl,' he said.

'I know.' She rolled her eyes. 'Whatever must you think of me?'

'Only good things.'

He adored that she was unashamed of her body and the pleasure that they'd had last night.

And Libby adored it that he did not mention her big revelation about her career or her possibly rather red eyes.

He reached for his phone and raised an eyebrow in surprise when he saw that it was after eight. Usually he would be at work by now.

'I'm late,' he said.

'Well, it's very lucky that you're the boss, then.'

'True.' He turned and looked at her. 'Are you late?'

'No. I'm meeting one agent at ten to be shown through.'

'Near here?'

'No, that's not till one.'

'You should have booked them the other way round.'

'Ah, but I didn't know I was going to be sleeping in your bed!' She gave him a smile. 'Goldilocks.'

'I don't know that one so well.'

'Well, I guess you'd have grown up on Russian ones.'

Daniil nodded and he thought for a moment of Sev reading to them, or Katya, the cook, who, when they had been little, would sometimes tell them a tale.

Nice memories, Daniil thought.

'I did,' he said, 'though where I come from the wolf is the good guy.'

'Really?'

'You've seen *Firebird*?'

'I've heard about it, of course, but, no, I've never actually seen it performed...'

'It's on in London now,' he said, and he waited for her to jump as most women would at the tiny line he'd just thrown them.

She didn't.

She lay there her in a state of self-imposed anxiety. Rachel, her flatmate, had been to see it twice and had suggested that Libby join her many times, until Libby had broken down and admitted that, no, she just couldn't face a full-scale production yet. Her head had let go of the dream, her heart just wasn't ready to, and it would hurt: it would be agonising to sit and watch what she now knew she would never be a part of again.

Daniil was relieved when she didn't jump. For a moment he considered taking her to the ballet but soon decided against it. He didn't want to give the false impression that this was about anything other than sex.

Still, it surprised him that he'd even considered it so he quickly changed the subject.

'Tell me more about your studios.'

'There's not much more to tell.'

'Have you spoken to the bank?'

Libby gave a small grimace. 'I'm doing that this afternoon.'

'Are you prepared for them?'

'I think so,' she said, and went a bit pink. 'Actually, last night I was going to sit down and work out figures.' She let out a sigh. 'I'd far rather talk about wolves…'

'I know that you would but you need to sort this out.'

'Do you always hold a business meeting with your lovers the next morning?'

'The scatty ones, yes,' he said, and didn't reveal that *any* conversation was rare the next morning. 'You are too vague. I think you are leaning towards the one in the East End and that would be a mistake.'

'Er, I have given this some thought. The one near here charges four times the rent. I can hardly quadruple my prices.'

'No, but if you can double your number of students you only have to charge double the fee. It's maths.'

'Perhaps but there's only one of me.'

'So you might get a senior to take some of the juniors.'

'Oh, so you're an expert in ballet?'

'No,' Daniil calmly responded to her slightly sarcastic tone. 'I'm an expert in business.'

She frowned. She'd have thought he only knew about massive conglomerates but as he spoke on, more and more it seemed that he understood what she would be dealing with if she opened her own dance school.

In fact, he hit several points that Libby had been hoping she could gloss over when she spoke with the bank.

'The poorer suburb that you are talking about—I doubt there would be a lot of spare money for dance classes and costumes.'

'Dance should be available to everyone.'

'Please.' Now it was Daniil who rolled his eyes. 'If that's your aim then go and hire a hall and give it away for free. What if you get a child with real talent and her parents can't afford the extra classes?'

Libby lay there.

She didn't have to tell him her answer. Of course, she would give the child free lessons—how could she not?

'Now,' Daniil continued, 'around here they could afford it. Even for the fat kid with no talent the parents will pay through the nose…'

He was cruel, he was abrasive but, damn him, he was right.

'Here you could hold adult classes during the day, lunchtime ones—people are trying to squeeze exercise into their days. What were the premises used as previously?'

'The one near here was used for yoga and the other a ballet and jazz school.'

'Ask the agents why they closed down. I know you

dismissed that yesterday but it is a very important question you must ask and take careful note of the answer.'

'I shall.'

'Are you putting your own savings into it?'

Libby's snort told him that she had none. 'No, just my talent and enthusiasm…' She let out a sigh. 'I haven't a hope with the bank.'

'Go and have a shower,' he said. 'I'll make a drink.'

He didn't join her.

Deliberately.

There was something about sex in the morning that was a touch too intimate for Daniil, but as she climbed out of bed and stretched again he wanted to break his own rule.

Even his bathroom was sexy, Libby thought as she stepped inside.

It wasn't warm and inviting, but it was decadent all the same.

It was tiled in white and one wall was a mirror, set back in the middle and angled so that she could see her body from every direction. No, it wasn't ballet exercises she envisaged as she stood there—instead, it was her and Daniil in this space.

Behind a glass wall were towels as thick as pillows. He had an array of toiletries and Libby spent a few giddy moments opening lids and inhaling his scent. At first she wondered where the shower was but when she flicked a button she soon found out that water came from a long rod set in the ceiling and shot in strong jets at her from every direction.

It was utter bliss and she stood for perhaps a while longer than one usually would in the circumstances and then she turned the water off and wrapped herself in one of his fluffy towels. She would have loved to have simply padded out and back to his bed.

Instead, she used all his lotions, not just for the luxurious feel of them on her skin and in her hair, more that for the entire day she would have a little of the scent of him.

'That,' Libby said, as she came into the kitchen, dressed as she had been last night but now all damp and pink, 'was the nicest shower I have ever had.'

'Good,' he said, handing her a drink.

He had made her a frothy coffee and Libby added sugar and saw that Daniil drank black tea with the bag still in the cup.

As she perched on a bar stool he stood leaning against a counter, and it was awkward between them for the first time.

'You should have take-out cups so that you can avoid the small talk,' Libby commented, and he even managed a small smile.

'I don't normally do coffee.'

'Well, I'll consider it a compliment, then,' she said. She made it halfway down her mug before the awkwardness became too much for her, and deciding that it really was time to go she hopped down from the bar stool. 'If I want to get there before ten, I'd better head off.'

Daniil waited for one of two questions—for Libby to ask if he'd given any more thought to attending his parents' anniversary celebration.

Or if they might see each other again.

'I can have you driven or a taxi,' Daniil offered.

'No, thanks,' she said, because that would mean she wouldn't need to leave for a while and it was already tense between them.

Why did it have to be like this? she wondered.

It just did.

She'd heeded the warnings and had gone into it with her eyes wide-open, if a touch dilated by lust. No, she didn't want him down on one knee, begging her not to go, but the ending of them was, for Libby, harder than she could ever have anticipated when she had accepted his invitation to bed.

'Thank you for a lovely evening,' she said. She came around the kitchen bench and whether he wanted one or not she gave him a kiss on his cheek.

Even his clenched jaw was sexy, she thought. She wanted to rub her lips over his rough chin but she restrained herself.

A bit.

Well, no, she didn't, she did exactly that. She wanted to coil around him and live on his hips, she thought as she inhaled his heady scent. She'd be no trouble at all, he could carry on with his day and just give her the odd glass of water and bar of chocolate.

'What's funny?' Daniil said, as she pulled her head back.

'The things that I think.'

She walked out with barely a sound and gave him a half-wave as she let herself out of the door and he stood there, waiting for her to turn around.

Oh, I was just wondering if you'd given it any more thought...

She didn't.

You know you mentioned Firebird, *well, maybe we could...*

She didn't suggest that they see each other again, either.

He heard the door close and at fifteen minutes to nine,

some fourteen hours and forty-five minutes after they had met, Libby Tennent was gone.

Libby sat on the underground on the way to her appointment with the estate agent.

She was back to reality but after last night she knew she was changed forever.

Oh, she knew her mother would faint if she told her what she had got up to and her sensible older sister probably would, too. Then again, they'd always thought she had her head on backwards.

And her father?

Well, he'd thoroughly disapprove, of course, and then after ten minutes of sulking would be wondering how it might benefit the family business.

She was sick of it.

Guilt ridden with it, too.

Yes, she had begged for extra lessons, for private tuition, and the business had, of course, funded that, but did it mean she now had to work for him, doing something she didn't love?

Had it all been conditional on her making it to number one for their investment in her to count?

Couldn't she just love what she did?

Coming out of the underground her phone rang and Libby saw that it was her father. She would have preferred not to have answered but given his accident yesterday she felt she ought to. 'How are you this morning?' Libby asked.

'Pretty bruised,' Lindsey said. 'Did you get anywhere at all with Zverev?'

'Nowhere,' she answered. Well, yes, technically she lied, but she was hardly going to let her father know just how far she'd actually gone! 'Dad, I think you've just got to accept that he isn't going to go...'

'But—'

'It's not up to us to persuade him, Dad,' Libby said, and she was firmer than she usually was with him. 'And if your entire business is reliant on him attending then I think you've got bigger things that need to be faced.'

'Elizabeth!'

'Well, it's true,' she said.

'If things go well with this then I'll be back in the game. And if you came on board...'

She closed her eyes as the same old argument was raised. They had never taken her dancing seriously, they had considered it a phase, an expensive hobby that they had indulged her in, and now it was time to pay them back.

'Libby, what are you doing, looking at dance schools when you're needed here? We've done all we can to support your dancing but clearly it hasn't worked out...'

The tiny paper cuts her family delivered over and over hurt.

Okay, maybe she hadn't made it to the top, maybe she'd never been cut out to be a soloist, but didn't any of her career count to them?

'Dancing still is my career.'

'Even when your family needs you? Look, if you can't help us out there then at least go and speak with Zverev again...use your charm, smile that smile.'

Now at least he was being a little more honest, though it had taken Daniil to get her to fully see that her father had been hoping that a woman might make more headway with Daniil than he could.

'It's not going to happen, Dad—I shan't be seeing

Daniil again. So maybe you should contact the Thomases and let them know that their son isn't going to be attending their anniversary celebration.'

Libby turned off the phone and got back to daydreaming about Daniil and trying to fathom how at twenty-five she'd possibly already had the best night of her life.

His little pep talk about business, however unwelcome at the time, did help today though.

The first studio she saw was perfect! There were huge mirrored walls and the floor space was amazing. There was a small kitchenette, a nice-size changing room…

'What happened to the last business?' Libby asked.

'I'm not sure.' The agent was evasive. 'I think she retired.'

Hmm.

Back to the Land of Daniil she went and met with the second agent.

This studio was smaller but the floor space was enough and there was also a little waiting area that hopefully she could lock the parents into so they didn't interfere!

'What happened to the last business?' Libby asked.

'Yoga,' the agent said. 'They moved to new premises, a converted warehouse, as they needed more space.'

Oh, it made sense to go there, but the bank wasn't going to listen to her, Libby was sure.

'I've got another woman coming for a second look tomorrow,' the agent said. 'She's very keen.'

Libby shrugged but her heart leaped in her throat.

She wanted this place very badly.

She thanked the agent and he locked up and got into his car and she stood awhile longer, peering through the window, desperate for her dream to live here.

'Well?'

She jumped at the sound of that gorgeous, low, chocolaty voice.

'Daniil!' She turned and gave him a wide smile. 'Shouldn't you be at work?'

'I have been,' he said, and then handed her a large creamy envelope with the Zverev name embossed in gold on the corner. 'This is for you.'

'Oh, God, did you mark my performance last night?' she exclaimed. 'Did my knees crack…?'

She made herself laugh but he didn't join her. 'It was a joke…' she started, but then her voice trailed off as she opened the envelope and read what was written.

'Oh, my!'

She had a business plan.

A real one.

It went into demographics of the area, mean ages, average incomes and things she'd never have thought of. He'd even put things like expected revenue from the vending machine that it looked as if she'd be getting and the cost of hiring mirrors.

Everything had been taken into account.

'I'm not asking for this much!' Libby yelped when she saw the figure he had suggested the bank give her for a loan.

'You don't have to spend it, but it is something to factor in if you get sick or you get so busy that you have to hire another teacher.'

There were pages and pages of it.

All the little throwaway stuff she'd told him, about her career, her study, was all neatly referenced and then he'd added that in his opinion the proposed business model was an extremely viable one and it was signed with his lovely expensive signature.

And that if they required more information, they could contact him.

Oh, my!

This would have cost her thousands to have done privately. In fact, it wouldn't have happened, because there was no way Daniil Zverev would have done this for her if she'd stepped in from the street.

Which she had.

Sort of.

'You'll get the loan.'

He sounded so sure that Libby was starting to believe that she would. That he had spent the morning doing this for her almost blew her away, but instead she put her arms around his neck and held on tight to the lovely anchor of him.

'I have to kiss you!'

He lifted her up so she could do so. He was just so big and strong and sexy as hell and his jaw less rigid than this morning as she ran her lips over it. His mouth was receptive, taking her kiss, returning it fiercely, but only for a moment because, though holding her, he peeled his face back from her liberal display of affection.

'Thank you,' Libby said.

'You're welcome.'

She didn't want to come back to planet earth but he placed her back on it.

'I have to go now.'

And just like that he did, leaving her standing there, reeling.

Excited, elated and back to the agony of his leaving, which was worse the second time around.

He'd broken their unspoken rule.

Libby had been set to get on with her life, to determinedly not contact him and to expect nothing more from their one night.

He'd given her more than a business plan, Libby thought.

Daniil Zverev had given her hope for them—that she might see him again, that last night had meant more to him, too.

And that was scary.

CHAPTER FIVE

DANIIL STARED AT the phone.

His mind was finally made up.

Almost.

He was leaning towards going to his parents' anniversary party, which was being held next weekend.

The ongoing pressure from Lindsey Tennent had had nothing to do with his change of heart. Lindsey had today called Reception twice, using different names, in an effort to be put through to him. One call had made it as far as Cindy but she had quickly seen through him.

Daniil re-read the invitation: *To Daniel Thomas*.

Reverting to his own name had been the final straw that had caused his parents to disown him. They had taken it as a personal affront and had said that, in doing so, he not only shamed them but it was a smack in the face for all they had done for him. They had refused to listen to his reasoning and, for Daniil, it had actually come as a relief when they had said that they wanted nothing more to do with him.

It had suited him, in fact.

The occasional visits he used to make at Christmas and for birthdays were excruciating at best, for all concerned. He could feel the strain from the moment he walked in and there was a sigh of relief that had reverberated from everyone when the duty visit was over and done, till the next time.

No, it wasn't a moral debt or his conscience that had Daniil changing his mind. He had a question for his parents and he wanted an honest answer. He might not get one, but he would be able to know if they were lying if the question was asked face to face.

Did you mail the letters I wrote to Roman?

He was sure that they hadn't, but that realisation had come a long time after the letters had been penned. At first Daniil had believed his parents when they had said that the post was very slow. They had also suggested, when still no letter had come, that maybe his brother was still angry at him and they would point to Daniil's cheek. That had made no sense because Daniil was quite sure now that the fight had been Roman's attempt to force him to leave the orphanage.

Only when he had left home and gone to university had Daniil considered that his parents may have lied and simply not mailed them. Of course, by then Roman had long since left the orphanage—to where, no one had been able to tell him.

Daniil actually felt as if a part of him was missing. A vital part—his identity.

He had been back to Russia on several occasions but had always drawn a blank. He was going again, for another attempt at finding out what had happened to his twin, after the anniversary.

He knew how much he missed his twin, and surely it must be the same for Roman. Daniil knew he would spend the rest of his life searching for him.

Yes, he had decided that he would go to the anniversary party and make the speech, just for the chance to get to the truth, but as he went to make the call his intercom buzzed and he heard his receptionist's resigned voice.

'There's a Ms Tennent in Reception, asking to see you. It's been explained to her that she doesn't have an appointment. She insists that we ask for ten minutes of your time.'

Daniil let out a slight curse.

Of course Libby was here.

No doubt Lindsey was sending in the big guns again.

Well, Libby could hardly be called a big gun.

'She can have five minutes.'

'Oh.'

Cindy was clearly expecting him to offer his usual refusal, and possibly he should have, but he had been waiting for a week for her to make contact and ask that he reconsider about the anniversary celebration.

There was, Daniil believed, always a hidden agenda and so far he had never been proved wrong.

'Cindy, you can go to lunch once she is here. Tell Libby that she can come straight through.'

He leaned back in his chair and waited.

It was almost a relief that her true colours would now reveal themselves because he hadn't been able to get her out of his head.

The business plan had been a spur-of-the-moment thing, and by that evening he had regretted it.

He had arrived home from work and as promised his back had felt as if he'd been run over by a bus.

It had felt the same for the next two days but on the third…

Yes, he had remembered fondly.

Extremely fondly, in fact, because he had had his first weekend in in very long time.

'Whoops!' Libby said as she burst into his office in a blaze of colour. 'I nearly knocked.'

Daniil sat there.

She was wearing a bright red wraparound dress that looked rather like a very tight T-shirt, bright red lipstick and her smile was wide.

She also had her huge leather bag over her shoulder.

'Guess where I've been?' Libby said.

'I have no idea.'

She made a great show of going into her bag, opening her purse and taking out a pale pink business card, and then she came around the desk and handed it to him.

Libby Tennent School of Dance

Beneath that was a photo of two lower legs in the same blush pink and the dancer was *en pointe*.

'Do you like it?' she asked. 'It took me hours, no, *days*, to sign off on it.'

He had never seen anyone so delighted with a business card. Daniil could fill a room with all the cards that had been handed to him over the years.

'You can keep it if you like,' she said, as he went to hand it back. 'I've got hundreds.'

As soon as she'd gone he would do his usual and toss it in the bin and for now he gave a polite nod, but the examination of the business card hadn't finished yet because she was standing over him, peering at it.

'It's gorgeous, isn't it?' she sighed, and then Daniil looked a little closer and, yes, it actually was because...

'That's you.'

There was a certain disquiet in Daniil that he could recognise her from the knees down!

'It is! Well, it's me two years ago. Are you going to guess where I've been?'

'No,' he said, because he didn't partake in games.

'Then, I'll tell you—I've just picked up the keys to the studio.' She beamed. 'And the mirrors are coming this afternoon. I've had a poster printed for my information evening... I'm just so happy and excited that I wanted to come and say thank you for all your help.'

Daniil stared as again she went into her bag.

'Here.' She pulled out a present, beautifully wrapped and tied with a pale pink satin bow, and there was a card addressed to him.

'What's this?'

'Well, if you open it you'll find out.'

Daniil didn't like gifts.

Birthdays at the orphanage had meant an extra piece of fruit with lunch and knuckles on the head from his peers. He had never received a wrapped gift, chosen specifically for him, until he had come to live in England and had quickly found out that always, *always*, they came with guilt or conditions attached.

He remembered getting a tennis racket when he hadn't liked the game and finding out later that their late son, Daniel, had been a gifted tennis player.

There had been clothes, books, instruments, computers and electronics, too, that had supposedly been chosen for him, but Daniil had known the thought had been with their late son.

At eighteen he had stood awkwardly as he'd been handed a bunch of keys and taken out to the drive where a luxury navy car sat wrapped in a bow. He had caused tears when he had refused to perform for the video camera and take his gift for a drive.

It hadn't been a gift in the true sense.

Daniil had known that again it would come at a price.

How grateful he should be, he had often been told. Didn't he understand just how lucky he was?

Lately his gifts had been of the serious corporate kind but they, too, had come with their own quiet sway.

He looked up to Libby, who was waiting expectantly for him to open her gift.

'Come on...' she urged, as he undid the ribbon.

'Too much pink,' he commented.

'You can never have too much pink,' she said, as he peeled back the paper. 'It's not very exciting,' she warned as he opened the box. 'Well, it's exciting to me but I just...' Her voice trailed off as her gift was revealed.

It was a porcelain, hard *thing*. A bit like a grey-silver bear with pieces of glittery wool stuck to it, and it had a smiling face and eyes.

He removed it from the paper and saw that it had very long legs with the ends dressed in pink ribboned ballet shoes.

He tried to stand it on his desk but Libby laughed.

'It sits on your bookshelf,' she explained, and put it at the end of the desk so that its long legs dangled over the edge. She looked around his office. 'You, Daniil, are lacking in knick-knacks.

He didn't like pointless things.

Daniil had never been attached to a thing for the sake of it.

And, yes, this was possibly the most pointless thing that had ever graced his desk.

'I've ordered loads,' Libby explained. 'I might give them as little prizes.'

'I see.'

He didn't.

'Well, I have to go,' Libby said. 'I've got to get back for my mirrors arriving...'

'What else did you want?'

'Nothing.' Libby beamed. 'Just to say thank you. I know now that I couldn't have done it without you. I tried by myself at the bank and I truly believe he was about to laugh me down the street when I produced your business plan. Honestly, almost the moment I did he offered me a coffee *and* I got two chocolate biscuits.'

Daniil looked at her and smiled. She, like the *thing*, was now sitting on his desk, only she was chatting away happily.

'How's your back?' Libby asked.

'Well, for a couple of days I struggled even to put a shirt on and if your ears were burning that was me, cursing your name every time I moved...'

'But then?' she said.

'Amazing,' Daniil said. 'If your ballet school flops you can—'

'Don't even say it!' she said. 'I'm terrified.'

'There's no need to be,' he said. 'I wouldn't put my name to any business plan that I didn't consider had every chance of succeeding.'

'Really?' She frowned. 'You weren't just being nice?'

'I don't lie about business,' he said. 'I was just being nice to you...'

'I didn't think you played nice,' she said, as he pulled her from the desk and onto his lap so that she was facing him.

'Occasionally I do,' he said, arranging her legs so she was half kneeling on the chair with her arms resting on his shoulders.

'I'd love to kiss you—' she sighed '—but I have far too much lipstick on for that.'

'Poor excuse.'

'Valid excuse,' she said. 'I really came just to give you your present. If they weren't going to let me up then I'd have left it with the misers at Reception. You haven't opened your card.'

'I will,' Daniil said. Right now, though, his hands were on her hips. 'Before you arrived I was about to call your father.'

'My father?' Libby blinked. 'And tell him what a bad girl his daughter is?'

'No.' Daniil smiled. 'To say that I will go next weekend.'

He waited for her smile to widen, for a dart of triumph in her eyes now that she had got her way, but he was slightly taken aback when instead she frowned.

'But you said that you didn't want to go.'

'I know that I did, but I've given it some thought and...' He wasn't about to tell her about the letters—that was way too personal to him—so he shrugged and was vague instead. 'Maybe it is the right thing to do.'

'Not if...' She was clearly uncomfortable with his choice. 'Daniil, I knew, almost the second I said I'd do it, that it was wrong to try to persuade you...'

'You didn't persuade me,' he said. 'I decided to go by myself.'

'You're sure?' she checked.

He nodded.

She was like no one he had ever met. He could tell that she was uncomfortable with her part in it all.

Up till that moment he had thought she might be playing a game and that the reason for her visit would contain another attempt to change his mind.

He moved her up his lap, just slithered her unresisting body closer to his.

'Someone might come in,' she said.

'No one ever comes in without Cindy's say-so.'

'Even so.'

But remembering that he had sent Cindy to lunch, Daniil went into his drawer and pulled out a tiny remote and there was the *thunk* of the door locking.

She wanted him but hadn't expected this.

For a week there had been nothing. No phone call, no flowers, no anything and now here she was, sitting on his lap facing him.

Their one night Libby could never describe as a mistake but, despite her bravado, it had rattled her.

A lot.

She had found it hard, no, impossible, to believe that was it and, guiltily, even if the present had been left at Reception she had hoped it might serve as a prompt, to remind him about what she could not forget—their night.

'I can't kiss you,' Libby said, revelling at the feel of his solid legs between her thighs. 'I'm not walking out of here with my face all smeared.'

'Don't…' He was about to say, 'Don't come here wearing red lipstick next time, then,' but changed his mind. 'Don't kiss me, then, but I can still kiss you.'

She closed her eyes in bliss as his lips met her neck and her skin nearly wept in relief as finally Houston made contact again. His lips brushed her tender skin and then there was the warm wet slide of tongue. As he kissed her neck he undid the wrap of her dress and then lowered the little cami she wore so one breast was exposed, and he kissed her there. He swirled round her nipple with his tongue, making little nips with his teeth.

'Oh...' Libby squirmed in his lap at the pleasure and held on to his shoulders. His tongue was cool on her breast at first and then warm, the tiny nips and sucks were making her feel faint and she was incredibly, rapidly, turned on, especially as he slid down in the seat enough so that his hands moved her hips over his erection.

'This could go far too far...' she breathed, as his fingers burrowed into her panties.

'Good.'

It did go far too far because he took a letter opener and dealt with the lacy threads of her underwear so she was completely naked to the hand that stroked her.

'Daniil...' she whispered into his ear, 'I'm not on the Pill...'

'Get yourself on it, then.'

She blinked.

She wanted to dash out and find where Cindy kept the fire extinguisher just so she could put out the sudden hope in her heart that flared. The hope that said that there would be more, that he and she...

'What?' he said, as he felt her still.

'I went to the doctor this morning. It's okay, I wasn't hanging out for you to call me or anything...' She hesitated and then, what the hell, she chose honesty. 'Well, of course I was, but really I was a little worried by my lack of morals the other night. I don't regularly fall into bed...'

'You didn't fall,' he said. 'I wouldn't let you.'

In between words he was flicking her nipple with his tongue and it felt as he was doing the same to her clitoris as she remembered her legs resting on his shoulders as he'd made magic with his mouth.

'The other night was…' Libby attempted to explain that it had been an exception but it was hard to form a sentence as his fingers moved faster inside her and the suction of his mouth around her breast had her frantic in his arms.

'Precious and rare,' Daniil finished the sentence for her in the nicest of ways.

'It was,' she said. 'So I am getting myself on the Pill the very second I can…'

'Come,' Daniil said, his fingers working her, 'and then we will see what you can do with that red mouth.'

She unbelted him just to feel him, and then his hand discontinued the delicious probe of her and her sob of frustration turned into a moan of pleasure as she freed him. Hard, erect, there was a bead of moisture at the tip that had her longing to lower her head, but instead she rose up a little, not just to his hand, which was back where she felt it belonged and bringing her closer to the boil, but her legs raised to have him nearer her heat.

Again he removed that skilled hand and guided her so that she hovered, and he stroked her now with the head of his cock and her lips twitched from the absence of his kiss.

'Condom…' she breathed, because she was fighting not to lower herself.

'I don't have any here.'

'Please.' Libby let out a half laugh of disbelief.

'Why would I have them at work?'

He surprised her.

Always.

He pulled her down onto him just a little way. 'I want to feel you come around me.'

'You might, though.'

'I have a lot of self-control…'

It was a risky game, but they were way past reading the fine print of the rule books. Yes, somewhere it would state that this was foolish at best, but the thought of him inside her unsheathed had Libby licking her lips. She'd never done it without a condom and she told him so.

'Nor me.'

'Just for a moment, then.'

He lowered her down, not all the way, and she let out a moan of both bliss and want.

He raised her and then lowered her again, watching his naked length being swallowed up and feeling the blissful wet warmth of her.

Then he pulled her hard down and watched her grimace.

'Come on, baby,' he said, thrusting into her. 'I won't last long.'

'Talk about pressure…' she said, but the only real pressure was building in her. He just moved her at his will. She was limp and compliant and then suddenly her spine felt rigid and she was shaking and her orgasm was so deep, so intense she cried out.

For Daniil, feeling her pleasure, her concentrated tightness around him was rapturous. Yes, he had self-control but even Libby felt the final swell and jerk of him just before he lifted her off. She held his shoulders and they both watched as he shot over her and her desire flickered back to life as he stroked himself empty, her hand coming down over his and their fingers mingling.

She'd never seen anything more sexy, never felt more adored, and in that moment she truly was.

His tongue was cold as he ignored the rule that had got them to this point and kissed her slack mouth and then they rested their foreheads on each other's.

'I want to curl up and go to sleep...' Libby admitted, but what she didn't admit was that she wanted to do that right there on his lap. She wanted the door to stay locked and the rest of the world to disappear and leave them alone.

Libby had never had such intense feelings for anyone— no man had ever moved her in the way that he did—but already he was peeling her off.

Her jelly legs moved to a stand and she looked down at her panties where they lay shredded on the floor.

'Come on,' he said, and at first she thought she was being shown the door but instead he took her into the adjoining bathroom and it was the lipstick he dealt with first because they were both wearing it. He wetted a cloth and discarded the evidence from her face and then he stripped her and they showered, kissing, kissing, kissing, washing each other, caring for each other. Then he turned off the taps and it was time to dress.

Now it was time for Daniil to pretend it was simply sex.

God, but he'd prefer that it was.

He loathed having somebody in his headspace, he dreaded letting another person get close.

She could feel the awkwardness descend and there was no frothy coffee this time, her marching orders were given.

'I am expecting a client...'

'Please don't make excuses,' she said, pulling on her

dress and trying to get her arm in, which wasn't very easy with a body that was damp. 'I'm going.'

Now there was regret.

There was embarrassment on Libby's part that she'd practically handed herself to him and also the knowledge that their behaviour had been risky.

On Daniil's part, there was unease that he might care about her.

It hurt to care and he avoided that at all costs.

She went through her bag, where thankfully she had fresh underwear and she pulled it on as Daniil selected a fresh shirt and suit.

She tied up her hair and, even though she could feel his impatience, she took her time putting on her lipstick so she could at least look as if nothing had taken place.

She did that odd little wave at the door and got his grim smile in return.

She had that same feeling of having stepped out of a movie theatre as she came out of his office. Cindy's desk was empty. Presumably she was at lunch and there was no sign of the client he was waiting for.

The worst thing about seeing him was the parting.

She never knew if this was it.

CHAPTER SIX

DANIIL DIDN'T CALL HER.

He woke one morning, more than a week after she had stopped by his office, and lay in his bed, thinking. He didn't like how at any given hour his mind drifted to her, how he worried about whether or not she was okay, how he lay there wondering what she was feeling and also how he had to fight himself not to get in touch.

So after several moments doing his best not to think about Libby he went out and poured himself a long glass of water and checked his phone and scrolled through contacts.

Tonight he would go out, he decided.

Libby Tennent had occupied way too much of his headspace of late.

He pulled on some shorts and went into the room he hadn't allowed her to go into.

No one came in here, not even his domestic. This was strictly his space and he took care of it himself.

It was more than a gym, it was his sanctuary. There were training mats, punch bags and weights. This morning he did consider going to the club that he went to on occasion—they knew nothing about him, there he was Dan the moody Russian.

There, he taught kids drills and could spar with others, but he didn't feel like seeing anyone today.

He warmed up and then took a rope and skipped till he would usually be panting for breath, then he worked on some rhythm drills but he could not focus.

His mind was elsewhere.

He looked at the ledge and there was the *thing* she had brought him and next to it… Daniil took a drink and then walked over and picked up a very old photo.

Twenty years old, because he had been ten when it had been taken.

There he was, a slight smile on his mouth, excited that Sergio had brought in the camera, and that he was having his first photo taken.

Roman was next to him, unsmiling, and Daniil could remember every word of the conversation.

'Come on, Roman,' Sergio had said. 'Smile, you're going to be famous. This photo will be worth a lot one day—The Zverev twins.'

'When do we get to fight?' Roman had asked. That had been all he'd wanted to know.

'Soon,' Sergio had said.

For it had been a case of drills, more drills.

Daniil put down the photo and then picked up the card Libby had given him. He hadn't read it while she'd been there, instead it had remained unopened after she had gone, but curiosity finally won and he opened the envelope.

Thank you for making my dreams a reality.
Libby

He read it several times, searching for the inference, the little trip of guilt, a demand for more.

Was she talking about the dance school or their night together?

He closed the card and went to put it back on the shelf and then he saw a little postscript she had written on the back of the card.

Both...

She had answered his question.

He could almost see her chewing her pen before adding it.

Yes, he wanted to call her.

Instead, he put on gloves and went to the punch bag and reminded himself why he would not.

He thought of the upcoming anniversary party.

His cousin would be there, of course, smarming up to them.

Daniil didn't give a toss about the inheritance, more it was the thought of that greedy, cruel man getting a free ride that galled him.

'Face it, Daniel,' George had often said. 'You just don't fit in.'

Daniil could hear his cousin's voice as he took his anger out on the punch bag.

From the day you got here Aunt Katherine realised her mistake.

Oh, the punch bag earned its keep this morning as he recalled George's words.

Have you noticed how she blanches when she introduces you as her son?

But the worst one, the one that still hurt even now, especially now, was the one that held him back from pursuing a relationship—*This used to be such a happy home until you came on the scene.*

Daniil well remembered the toxic atmosphere of home—his mother's frequent tears and his father berating him for not living up to their son's ghost. He believed to this day what George had said—that the house, until he had arrived, had been a happy one, that it had been he who had caused all the pain.

He took out his anger on the punch bag till he was physically exhausted but with his mind still racing. He could not stand the thought of dimming the light in the star that Libby was.

He drove to work and took a slight detour. Slowing down, he saw a large pink poster and discovered that between four and seven she was holding an information evening.

Tonight.

Fortunately he had a very important dinner meeting tonight because still, despite a workout, despite the knot of dread at going to his parents' at the weekend, there was the temptation to make contact.

Getting too close to anyone was something he avoided at all costs and yet Libby had simply stepped over the walls he had put up. Direct as she was, he never felt invaded and, he thought, she made him smile.

He made her smile, too, Daniil realised as he drove on. She had walked into his office, and the closer she had got to his desk the wider her smile had become.

She seemed happy when she was with him.

For the first time Daniil was considering that he might make somebody happy.

Libby should be at her happiest, she well knew.

The turnout for the information evening had surpassed her expectations—parents had brought their children, lots of women had come to find out about classes during the day and some had suggested she hold a class once or twice a week later into the evening, so that they could come once the children were in bed. A young girl called Sonia, Libby was particularly impressed with. She was fifteen years old and very talented, and was looking for an opportunity for part-time work.

Libby had thought it would be a very long time before she could even consider hiring someone but, given the impressive turnout, she had told Sonia to come along next week so that she could speak to her one on one. For now she took out the garbage and came back in and smiled when she saw that she had only three little pink cupcakes left. She had bought loads but at first, not wanting to look presumptuous, she had only put out a small plate. The rest of them she had hidden in the little kitchenette.

Presumptuous.

Yes, that word was the reason why, even during her busiest most exhilarating week, she couldn't quite hit happy.

Oh, she'd tried not to get her hopes up, or to assume that he'd call, but such was their chemistry she just couldn't believe how easily he could let her go.

She'd given him a business card, for God's sake, so it wasn't as if he didn't have her number.

Worse, Libby knew that she had made things far too easy for him.

She should have left the present at Reception. Yes, she had practically handed herself to him with a pink satin bow on top.

Maybe he thought she was easy?

Well, so was he!

She angrily pulled down the blinds, terribly cross with herself.

The writing had been on the wall from the start and she had chosen to ignore it.

What had she expected? For man like Daniil to send flowers with a little love note?

Hell, yes!

As she turned Libby saw a broad shadow at the door and realised it was him. He'd startled her so much that instead of opening up Libby pulled down the blind on the door.

'We're closed,' she said. 'The information night finished at seven.'

'Libby…' He opened the letterbox and spoke through it. 'It's me.'

She said nothing.

'I think we both know that I'm not here for a ballet lesson,' he said.

She shouldn't open the door—it was as simple as that, she knew. She should tell him to go away. While she was thrilled that he had turned up, a week between meetings was far too long.

'Libby?' Daniil pushed open the letterbox and his voice was as if he was there in the studio. 'Are you going to let me in?' His answer was hearing the lock release on the door.

Libby thought, *Why does he have to be so beautiful?* With just one look at him she felt like melting but she remained firm with herself.

'I assume you're not here for a cupcake? I have three left,' she said, rabbiting on as he stepped in. 'Honestly, I thought I'd have to freeze them and that Rachel and I would be living off them for weeks.'

'Rachel?' Daniil checked.

'She's my flatmate,' Libby said.

'Another dancer?' Daniil checked, and she nodded.

'So if you're not here for a cupcake then what are you here for?' Libby said. And then answered her own question. 'Oh, I know—sex!'

'What the hell is that supposed to mean?'

'Well, given that this is almost within walking distance from the office, I guess it might make things easier for you. If you suddenly get bored in your lunch break...'

'Stop right there,' he said, and looked at her. She was wearing a dark purple dance outfit, with leggings over the top, and though similar to the woman he had met just a couple of weeks ago she looked tired now. He could see that there were dark circles under her eyes and that she was paler than she had been before.

He knew that she had been busy and had every right to look tired but he acknowledged the certain fact that some of the sleeplessness might be down to him.

He wasn't being arrogant. Daniil had spent many hours awake himself, willing himself not to get in touch, not to tarnish her world, and now he was here, about to ask a favour—for her to come to his parents' with him.

He couldn't do it, though.

'I was just wondering how your information evening went,' he said instead.

'Well, if you want to discuss my business, you can make an appointment,' Libby said, stuffing all her belongings into her bag, determined to just lock up and go home.

'Libby...'

He came over and she was on her knees, looking up at him. 'I don't for one minute believe that that's the reason you're here.' She looked up at his groin. 'Are you disappointed that you didn't get everything you wanted the other day?'

He had the gall to laugh. 'I'm actually on my way to a dinner meeting. I'm already running late.'

'Oh, I'm sure they'll wait for *you* to suddenly appear!'

He heard the barb, and one of the things he adored about her was that, just in case he'd missed it, she made very sure he got her point.

'I mean, we're all supposed to be happy to idly wait for you to drop by. Am I not even worth a single bunch of flowers?' she asked, as she angrily stood up.

'Libby,' Daniil said. 'I have never sent flowers in my life.'

'If I hadn't come to your office I'm quite sure that I'd never have seen you again.'

'Exactly. *You* came by *my* office! You took it further.'

Libby furiously shook her head. 'Daniil, you broke the rules. You were the one who turned up out of the blue the next day with a business plan for me. If you'd just left it at one night then I'd have known where I stood. Now I don't have a clue. You don't call me, you don't text...'

'What is it with women and texting?' he asked.

'It's nice to know that you're being thought of.'

'I never took you for needy.'

'I never took myself for a slut,' Libby said. 'But when you frogmarched me out of the office after we'd had sex, that was what I became.'

'Please.' He scoffed at her exaggeration, but he did relent just a touch. 'I was uncomfortable,' he admitted. 'I never bring my personal life to work.'

Libby was dubious. From what she'd read, he was at

it all the time but then she did remember that there had been no condoms to hand.

'What about Cindy?' Libby asked.

'Her husband is twice my size and three times as miserable.'

'What about your clients?' She simply had to know more about him, about his world, about what she was dealing with.

'Most are portly middle-aged businessmen.' Daniil shrugged. 'If I want sex I go out. I don't bring my personal life to work.'

She got that what had happened had been a rarity but, still, the endless stretches of silence from him galled and she told him that.

'I said from the start—'

'You did,' she responded, 'and maybe when you offered your little warning about not expecting you to love me I should have offered you a warning of my own—if you're involved with me, then you're involved. I'm not dangling on for weeks, wondering if you're going to call.'

'Fine,' Daniil said. 'I won't be calling. So now you know.'

'Or drop in on me unannounced.'

'Very well,' Daniil said. 'I shan't do so again.'

She wanted to stamp her feet in frustration as he complied with wishes she didn't really want and so she pushed him instead, pressing one hand up against his broad chest. She might as well have been a fly for all the impact she had. 'You make me so cross.'

'I know I do.' He shrugged. 'Tell you what, why don't you come with me tonight?'

'To dinner?'

'No.' He shook his head. 'It's going to be a very long,

boring meal and there are no partners allowed given that all we'll be doing is talking business. I do, though, have a suite booked.'

'Oh, I bet that you do,' she sneered.

'I won't lay a finger on you,' Daniil said. 'You could have a sleep or order room service, maybe have a massage or even just spend the night in the bath.' He smiled as her rapid blink indicated that the last suggestion was the one that tempted her most. 'They have a bath menu...' Daniil said.

'Really?'

'Really.'

'Is that what you came here for?' Libby asked. 'To ask me to come with you tonight?'

'No.'

'Then, why are you asking me now?'

'You bring out the niceness in me,' he said. 'You look tired. It might be pleasant to be spoiled. My driver can take you home or back here tomorrow.'

Libby stared back at him and thought of the frozen meal waiting for her in the freezer at home after a long ride on the underground. And then she thought of another long ride on the underground to get back here tomorrow.

Then she thought of a bath in a luxury hotel suite, room service and the bliss of having his driver in the morning.

And then she thought of one more night in his arms.

She didn't for a second believe that he wouldn't touch her.

He watched her eyes as all those thoughts raced through her head and he guessed exactly the moment she decided to accept, because she gave him an angry look.

How she wished she could be a little more haughty

and aloof and say no to him, but instead her shoulders sagged in defeat. 'Yes,' she said, and gave his chest another push. 'I'm still cross, though.'

'I know you are.' He didn't try to change her mind. 'You lock up and I'll wait in the car.'

Yes, she was cross, Libby thought, but there she went dreaming and hoping again because after all he had come around.

The drive was a short one and they were soon at the hotel. Of course, Daniil didn't have to worry about checking in the way mere mortals did. He was greeted with a handshake and taken straight up to his suite.

As she stepped in it wasn't the huge bed or the luxurious surroundings that made a shiver run down her spine—yes, things in Daniil's world certainly moved quickly because he picked up, from a walnut table, a huge bouquet of the palest pink peonies, roses and calla lilies and handed them to her.

There was even a card!

It took a week to find the perfect blooms—Daniil

'I don't believe it took a week,' she said, but gave a little *humph* noise, because the blooms were so perfect and her favourite colour. Possibly she could pretend it had taken him a week to find them and that he hadn't ordered them from the car while she'd locked up.

'I can be thoughtful when pushed,' he said, and she buried her face in the flowers when she wanted her hand back on his chest, but for different reasons this time.

She put the flowers in the huge vase that had been put on the table but she moved them through to the stunning bedroom and placed them by the side of the bed.

'You shouldn't sleep with flowers in the bedroom,' Daniil said.

'Sleep out there, then,' she said, because she wasn't letting the flowers out of her sight. She sat on the bed and it was like sinking into a marshmallow, and she watched Daniil as he quickly went through some notes on his computer.

'I was supposed to be doing this on the way here,' he admitted, and then glanced over to where she sat happily watching him, content to let him do whatever he had to. 'Will you be bored?' he checked.

'I hope so,' Libby sighed. 'That's my ambition.'

'Right,' he said. 'I'm going to go down. Wish me luck?'

'For a business dinner?'

'More than that,' he said. 'I want to buy this place.'

'Don't I get a kiss?' she asked, as he went to leave.

'I promised not to lay a finger on you.'

'Just your lips, then.'

'Nope,' he said, and then he was gone.

Libby lay back on the bed, breathing in the scent of the flowers, with the feeling that the world seemed in better order now.

She looked out of the window. There was her friend Big Ben and she remembered giving Daniil a massage, wishing she could freeze the hands of time.

And here she was again.

She had a bath and she deviated from the menu with a request of petals of her own—pale pink peonies and roses and calla lilies.

Damn the man. Till now anemones had been her favourite flower, which had been good because they were cheap.

Now, as she lay in her lovely bath with room service on

the way, she pictured a life with half her wages spent on luxurious flowers just so she could remember this bliss.

Daniil had spent a lot of time trying to convince himself that it was because the sex was good between them that he kept going back to her.

But as dinner dragged on his theory worked less and less.

He could not stop thinking about her, wondering what she was doing in the suite, thinking back to their conversation and her demand for a text. He was actually considering sending one; he had her business card in his wallet and he could easily pause the conversation and do just that.

No.

He was seriously considering buying this place—he should have his mind more on the conversation.

It usually was.

Daniil never mixed business with pleasure—his mind was only ever on one thing at a time.

Tonight, though, his thoughts kept drifting several floors up. He was glad that he had brought Libby and it felt good to know that after this very long dinner meeting he could simply head upstairs to her.

No, he did not want a brandy. In fact, he drank his coffee down in one and wished the current owners goodnight.

Just after midnight he arrived at the penthouse suite.

The maid was wheeling away the trolley and he halted her. He lifted the lid on the plates and there were the dark remains of a chocolate soufflé and also another dish that looked as if it had once held ice cream.

Good for her, Daniil thought. He was glad she was making the most of the night.

He stepped quietly into the suite and the air smelled fragrant, even more so in the bedroom. For a small moment he thought she must have gone home because in the darkness the bed, though unmade, looked empty, but there, he soon realised, she was—curled up in a ball and sound asleep.

No, Daniil knew for certain then that it wasn't sex that kept leading him back to her. She needed to sleep; he had seen how tired she'd looked tonight and for the first time in his life he undressed with the sole intention of not waking someone up.

He got into bed and the sigh she gave as she turned and curled into him was one of pure pleasure. He took her into his arms.

'I had the very best night...' Libby mumbled.

She had. It had been a completely indulgent night and it was better for knowing that he would soon join her. She was floaty and relaxed for the first time in... As his arms wrapped around her Libby lay there in a sugary haze, trying to remember how long it had been since she had felt this content and peaceful.

Since he had arrived in her life and turned it upside down?

No, because before then she had been grappling with the end of her dancing career and coming to terms with the fact that her performing days were over.

Before then, perhaps? No, because she had been grappling with her career just to stay in it.

And before then?

She had never known peace as if it was the answer.

'Go to sleep,' Daniil said, and kissed the top of her head, and she did just that.

It was a deep and dreamless sleep for both of them until just before dawn when Libby awoke in slight panic as his arms pulled her closer into him.

It didn't reassure her.

He'd be gone soon.

Libby had considered herself fully warned.

She hadn't thought that she might fall in love.

It was then she was honest with herself and admitted that she had done just that.

She was in love with Daniil Zverev, heartbreaker to the stars.

'You're okay,' he said, as if he understood a sudden panic.

He did.

Daniil had woken on many occasions thinking of Roman and wondering where the hell he was in this world and how he himself could even stand to be on the planet without him.

In more recent days he had lain filled with dread at the thought of a night back at his parents'.

He could barely stand the thought of going there—he knew that it would be hell. He felt her start to relax in his arms and her breathing evened out. She rested her head on his chest. He thought how much more pleasant the evening had been, simply knowing that she was near and that when the meeting was over she would be there.

Yes, it was far more than sex.

Daniil had never asked for help with anything in his life. In fact, he considered it selfish that he was even considering putting her through the misery of Saturday night just to make things easier on him.

But, selfishly, he was.

He needed her there.

'This weekend,' Daniil said into the darkness, 'does your father have to be there?'

Libby frowned as she pondered the question. 'I guess.'

'Could he stay away?'

'Why?'

'I want you to come with me.' He felt the flutter of her eyelashes on his chest as her eyes opened and he was grateful that she did not lift her head to look at him.

He couldn't quite admit just how much he wanted her there or how important it was to him, so he tried to keep things light.

'I want to take you because you know about my name change and things…'

'Of course,' she said, and then nodded. 'I'll speak to my father.'

Hope, foolish hope wasn't just unfurling in her chest, it ran like magical ivy through her body, and she tried to contain it, to tell herself he wasn't exactly taking her home to meet the parents, but she was sure there was more to it than that she knew of his name change.

'You'll go?' Daniil checked.

'I shall.'

It was then that she lifted her head and he lowered his and their mouths met and the kiss that they shared was different from any either had known—slow at first and then gently building…

Yes, it wasn't just about sex because, on this morning, they made love.

CHAPTER SEVEN

'I THOUGHT THAT you weren't going to get your hopes up,' Rachel commented as Libby packed her brand-new overnight bag. Her blond hair was in ringlets, her smile painted wide and every sentence seemed peppered by the word *Daniil*.

'Well, I'm trying my best not to,' Libby admitted, and then said to Rachel what she kept trying to tell herself. 'I don't think that this is a meet-the-parents night. I know that I'm just there because I...' She gave a little shake of the head rather than carry on speaking. Usually she told Rachel everything. They were very close friends, but she didn't feel quite right sharing Daniil's life. He was so intensely private that there wasn't much she knew, but the little he had told her felt like a gift.

'So it's an overnight thing?' Rachel asked, but Libby shrugged.

'I don't really know,' she admitted.

'Can't you call him and find out?'

'I don't have his phone number,' Libby sighed. 'Which is probably wise of him. I'd have found ten million reasons to text or call.'

Still, she lived in a state of suspension.

She knew she had gone a little bit overboard for tonight. She'd had her hair done and had bought everything new—right down to her toothbrush, which she was packing in her new toiletry bag.

'You know his reputation,' Rachel said.

'I do,' she called over her shoulder as she popped into the bathroom to grab her pills. 'I'm choosing to ignore it and just live in the now.'

And right now she was happy.

Terribly so.

Hopefully, Libby thought as she swiped her pills from the shelf, her period would wait until after the weekend was over and then she could start on them. It had been his comment about going on the Pill that had first given her hope and now that she was going to meet his family.

The one-night stand had spread over days and was starting to run into weeks. 'It's lasted far longer than I expected it to,' Libby said, as she wriggled into neutral sheer stockings and put on her brand-new dress.

'But you still don't have his number?'

'No.'

She headed to the lounge where the flowers he had bought her held prime position. They weren't exactly in pristine condition—the roses were open and splendid and, yes, the lilies were dropping pollen, but they were still a sight to behold.

'You should play it a bit more aloof,' Rachel warned, as Libby sat on the window ledge like a cat, watching the street and waiting for his car to appear.

'I know that I should but then I'd be lying to us both,' Libby said. 'Anyway, I've tried to play it all cool with him but I simply can't—the very second that I see him my self-control is shot. I've decided that I'm just going to be myself,' she said. 'It's all I can be.'

'Well, don't say I didn't warn you...' Rachel said, as a low silver sports car pulled up and a male model got out.

Actually, it was Daniil!

No, there was absolutely no such thing as playing it aloof where he was concerned. Libby answered the door before he had even knocked and as it opened Daniil, who was not looking forward to tonight, smiled at her effusive greeting.

'You look amazing,' Libby said, running her hands over his jacket simply to feel him. He was always immaculately dressed but tonight his black suit sat so beautifully on his shoulders and his crisp white shirt and gunmetal tie enhanced his beauty. Above his right eye was a small bruise and she ran a finger over it.

'Fighting again,' she commented, as she remembered the bruises on his chest the night they had met.

'Maybe I walked into a door.'

'Poor door,' she said, and his smile made her melt because she could feel that he was pleased to see her, also.

Of course, his greeting wasn't quite as over the top. 'You look very nice, too,' he said.

She would hope so!

'It's all new!' She gave him a twirl to show off her lovely moss-green dress. He then watched as she picked up some black court shoes and peeled the labels off before putting them on her feet.

'New shoes, too!'

'I told you it's *all* new.' She grinned and wrapped her arms around his neck. 'Now I can reach you.' His hands moved around her waist, stealing kisses between her words. 'New toothbrush, new overnight bag...'

'The loan went in, then?'

'It did!' Libby grinned again. 'However, this was a necessary expenditure…'

'Very necessary,' he agreed, because had her flatmate not been standing scowling at them he'd have been asking which way her bedroom was.

She was just so scented and dressed up and excited to see him and Daniil had never stepped into a home and felt so welcome.

Not once.

His home was always his chosen venue and hotel rooms, however luxurious they were, were bland at best.

Home had never been where the heart was for him and yet he could tell that happiness resided here and he was being welcomed in.

'Come through,' Libby said. 'This is Rachel.'

'Hi, Daniil,' Rachel said, and then looked straight at her friend. 'I hate you.'

'I know you do.' Libby smiled and led him through a door. 'This is the living room.'

He had a look around. They certainly did a lot of living in here—there were books and magazines and more *things* on every shelf space than he had ever seen.

The tour wasn't over yet.

'Kitchen.' Libby gestured as they passed it, though didn't stop to let him peek in. 'And there's the loo just in case you get lost in the dark at night.'

Oh, stop it, she told herself, but she could not contain her joy at having him there.

'And this,' Libby said, as they approached a door, 'is my bedroom.' As she went to open it he halted her hand.

'I'm guessing there's a theme,' he said. 'Pink?'

'Nope,' Libby said, and it was he who opened the door and stepped in.

There was no room for it to be pink.

He stepped into the chaos.

Usually he didn't like clutter, he didn't like anything out on display, and yet here in this room her whole life was on show.

There was a huge mirror where no doubt she exercised and there were endless pictures of her that had been taken through her dancing years. There were certificates on every wall—so much stuff he wondered how she ever found anything.

'I'm such a narcissist,' Libby said, as he looked closely at a huge framed photo of her.

'You're too nice to be one,' he said. 'Too thoughtful.'

'Well, I did tidy up for you,' Libby said.

'Really?'

'And I changed the sheets.'

'Are they new, too?'

Libby nodded. 'There was a selfish motive there, too, though...'

'Come on.' He smiled and released her. 'We had better go.'

He made no attempt to kiss her, Libby thought. Instead, he picked up her overnight bag and they headed out to his car.

'No driver?'

'Not at weekends.'

Into the passenger side she went and sank into the leather seat. The traffic was quieter than Daniil had allowed for and they were soon pulling into the parking basement of his office.

'Why are we here?' Libby asked.

She really didn't know anything about tonight.

'Because,' Daniil explained, 'on the rooftop there is a helipad.'

'Oh!' She had never been in a helicopter before. 'Are we flying back tonight?'

'I think we are expected to stay but I am going to keep the pilot on standby all night. I really don't know how it is going to go.'

They took the elevator to the foyer, Libby's shoes clipping away, making a noise on the marble floor, and, no, it didn't annoy him.

'We just have to stop in my office for a moment. I need to pick up the gift.'

'What did you get them?' she asked. He didn't answer at first and when they were in his office Libby blushed as she remembered what they had got up to at the desk.

'I'm not sure what Cindy got for them,' Daniil answered, and pointed to a large beautifully wrapped gift and picked up a note beside it. 'A ruby vase apparently.'

'A ruby vase?' Libby groaned. 'Have you no imagination?'

'I don't. Well, at least not where my parents are concerned, and Cindy certainly doesn't have one.'

'You sent her out to get your parents their gift?'

'Of course I did.'

Libby, who could happily spend a day thinking about the perfect gift for somebody, was appalled and suddenly terribly concerned about what had happened to the present she had bought him. 'Where's the present that I got for you?' she asked.

'I think it's in my drawer,' he said, and then watched as she opened it up and rummaged through for a full minute.

'No, it isn't.'

Daniil stood there as she opened his drawer, surprised

by his own non-reaction. Had anybody else done the same he might possibly have had their hands off.

'I don't know where it is, then,' he said. 'The cleaner must have moved it.'

Libby pouted. She didn't believe him for a moment. 'Should we go up?' she asked.

'We'll just wait here,' he said. 'I'll get a text when he's ready for us.'

Daniil walked over to the window and looked out at the bright late-afternoon sunshine and Libby could see the tension in his shoulders. 'Are you nervous about tonight?'

'I'm not nervous…' he said in a rather scoffing voice, but then he checked himself. It wasn't her fault how he felt right now. He had woken early this morning and taken himself to his club in the East End, where he had trained hard and then sparred, yet it had done little to relieve his mounting tension. That was the reason for the bruise over his eye and he was glad that Libby hadn't demanded answers. No, *nervous* wasn't the word and he tried to find the right one. He did not turn and look as he told her exactly how he felt. 'Dread.'

Libby, who was perched on his desk, felt the happy bubble she was floating on deflate on his behalf. 'I'm such a selfish cow,' she said, jumping off the desk and going over to him. 'I was so excited to see you that I never stopped to think just how hard this—'

'It's fine,' he interrupted. There was no need for an apology and he told her another truth. 'Despite how things are, I was looking forward to seeing you, too.'

For Libby, his open admission was unexpected.

It felt like opening the kitchen cupboard and finding a bar of chocolate when you were quite sure that you didn't have any.

And then Daniil elaborated on why he was dreading tonight and that, too, was unexpected. 'I'd better give you some background.'

'You don't have to,' she said, because she could sense his reluctance. 'I'm very good at winging it.'

'I'm going to be making a speech tonight so you will hear some of it anyway and I want you to know, before we arrive, why the evening might not be an easy one,' he said. 'As you know, I'm adopted.'

Libby nodded.

'I lived in an orphanage until I was twelve years old. Apparently my parents had tried for a very long time to have a baby and eventually they did—they had a son and his name was Daniel. He was their only child but he died when he was twelve and they missed him so much…'

Libby bit her tongue.

'They had hoped I would be like him. The trouble was, not only did I not speak the language—' he gave an extremely uncomfortable shrug '—I was very institutionalised when I arrived in England. I liked routines. Even though I was used to sharing a room, we all had our privacy. No one really touched anybody else's things. If someone was quiet, that was respected. It was very different when I came here. My parents felt they could come uninvited into my space, that they, or their maids, could touch my things. I wanted my meals at a certain time, that was all I knew. I didn't want their lavish food and to be grateful for the nice things they gave me. I didn't want to play tennis…'

He had wanted to box; that had been all he had wanted to do. If they had taken in Roman, he would have picked up a racket and shone at tennis, he would have been the perfect *Daniel*—but that part was too hard to share. And so, leaving his twin aside, as he had been forced to do for close to two-thirds of his life, Daniil told her a little more.

'I think that within a couple of days of me arriving they understood the mistake they had made. They wanted to love me but they couldn't and I don't blame them for that...'

Libby had kept hold of her mounting horror till now, but, as she had freely admitted, she had no self-control where Daniil was concerned. That someone could do that to him had her blood boil, and her voice was harsh when she spoke. 'They were never going to love you, no matter what you did. Instead of working through their grief and facing it, they did this to you.'

'I made their lives hell,' Daniil said. 'They simply couldn't understand how I wasn't grateful for all the opportunities they gave me. Earlier this year we had a major falling out when I told them I wanted to change back to my birth name.'

'Of course you did,' Libby said. 'After all they did—'

But he interrupted her, and when he did so Daniil nearly blindsided her with something she had never considered.

'I think they think that I changed my name to spite them—it wasn't about that, though. I changed my name in the hope that my past could find me.'

'And has it?'

'No.'

'I feel even worse now that I tried to persuade you to go.'

'Libby, you could never have persuaded me to do this. Believe me, I have my own reasons for going tonight.' He had revealed more than he ever had and certainly more than he had expected to, but her acceptance was sooth-

ing and that she was angry with his parents on his behalf helped. So a couple of hours before he would enter
the house that should have been home, he told her a little
of his real one.

'There were four of us,' he explained. 'We were the bad
kids. By the time you get to be six or so you know that you
are unlikely to be adopted. We never wanted to be anyway.
We were going to make our own way in the world. Sev—
Sevastyan—would read all the time, and he was clever
with numbers. Then there was Nikolai and he wanted to
work on the ships. I'd love to know if he ever did.'

'Who was the fourth one?' Libby asked innocently.

'Roman.'

It hurt even to say his name out loud.

'And what was he going to do?' Libby asked, but
Daniil just gave the same shake of his head that he
did when things were off limits, and finally his phone
bleeped a text and they could head to the roof.

But Libby halted him.

'You can still change your mind about going tonight.'

Not going was no longer an option. 'I have a question
for them,' he said. 'I hope that if I do the right thing by
them tonight they will give me an honest answer.'

'Isn't there a risk that they won't?'

'There are always risks,' he said. 'I only take them
if I am prepared to weather the consequences, and tonight I am.'

He was.

He wanted to know what had happened to the letters
he had sent, and if attending tonight gave him a chance
to find out, it was a price he was willing to pay.

Even if killed him to do so.

CHAPTER EIGHT

LIBBY KNEW THAT the view from the helicopter would be amazing but as it lifted into the sky she found that she was holding her breath. It was nerve-racking, dizzying and very unsettling. The buildings were getting smaller but, for a moment, she felt as if the ground was slamming upwards towards them. As the helicopter lurched a touch, so, too, did her stomach, and Libby discovered that possibly she wasn't suited to helicopters at all.

She swallowed the gathering saliva and then dragged in air and closed her eyes, appalled that she might be sick, but then Daniil placed his hand over hers and when next she opened her eyes the ground was back where it should be. The houses and flats were tiny and the landscape was becoming a deep gorgeous green as the helicopter headed towards Oxford. Libby looked over at Daniil and he mouthed that she would fine and she gave him a nod of thanks.

Would *he* be fine, though?

She was somehow trying to get her head around all that Daniil had told her. She tried to imagine arriving here, not knowing anything about the country and being unable to speak the language. She tried to understand how he must have felt, being sent in as some sort of replacement for a deceased child. For all her family's faults, for all the problems they might have, their love for each other had never been brought into question.

Through the headphones Libby heard the pilot announce their imminent arrival and saw Daniil staring out of the window, looking down to the vast expanse of land that held his home. His face was unreadable and her hand had been long forgotten. She glanced down and saw that he had clenched fists.

He was so closed off now that she might, Libby thought, just as well not be here.

Daniil couldn't really process that she was with him— till now he had always taken this journey alone. Yes, his new parents had sat beside him in the car the first time that his new home had come into view but they had been strangers then.

They still were.

For family occasions, his cousin's weddings included, he had never considered bringing a date. Through his teenage years and university not once had he thought of bringing somebody to the family home.

The sinking feeling he felt had nothing to do with the helicopter that was now hovering just before landing. He looked at the familiar red-brick mansion and the immaculate grounds that could all be his.

No, thank you.

He'd never once wanted to be here.

Daniil was almost tempted to ask the helicopter pilot to return them to London—in fact, he was seriously considering it—but just then he felt Libby's hand close over the top of his fingers and as he had sensed her nervousness earlier and reassured her, now she did the same to him. Daniil turned to smiling blue eyes that told him she was there, and that in a few short hours it would all be over and duty would be done.

It was he who nodded his thanks now.

They disembarked and the grass was so thick and lush that Libby wished she'd had the foresight to wear flats. Instead, she sank into the green carpet with each and every step till she gave in and took her heels off.

'Next time—' she started, but Daniil offered a swift retort.

'There won't be a next time.'

She tried to tell herself he was referring to the fact that they wouldn't come back to his parents' home but his comment still jarred. Daniil could be so brusque with his words that she never quite knew how they applied to her, or even if they did.

He didn't hold her hand as they walked up the stone steps, which she took as an affront, but Daniil was so tense he knew that if he did he might well crush her fingers. Everything about the place made him feel ill, from the growling stone lions to the fountain.

There was one familiar face that drew a pale smile from him—Marcus, the old butler who had been with the family since before his parents had married, opened the door. 'It's good to see you here, sir.'

'It's…' Yes, Daniil's response was initially sparse, he could hardly say that it was good to be here, but, determined to keep to his side of the deal, he pushed on. 'It's good to see you again, Marcus.'

'I'll have your luggage taken to your room,' Marcus said, and Daniil felt his stomach clench.

'I'd prefer—'

'Naturally, I'll leave it for you and your guest to unpack.'

Daniil gave a small nod of thanks, grateful that there was one person in this place who had, over the years, listened to his repeated requests that his belongings be left alone.

The entrance hall was as uninviting as it had been his first time here. At twelve he had been used to being surrounded by people and sparse furnishings. He would never forget first seeing this vast, imposing space, the walls lined with tapestries and portraits and the daunting Jacobean oak staircase. Most confusing of all had been that there were so few people.

'Daniel!'

Libby turned when she heard the *wrong* name and saw a small, busy-looking woman, with wiry hair and cold blue eyes, approach. She was wearing a deep red dress, which did nothing for her flushed complexion.

'Finally!'

Libby watched as she forced a smile, even though her lips seemed to disappear as she did so, and then a tall bearded man with a glass in his hand came and joined them.

'This is Libby,' Daniil said. 'Libby, this is my mother, Katherine, and my father, Richard.'

'It's lovely to meet you.' Libby beamed as they were introduced and no one, not even Daniil, could have guessed just how well she was acting right now, because from everything he had told her about them, there was no reason to smile.

Katherine ran her eyes over Libby, from head to toe and back again, and to Libby it felt as if she was being checked for lice. 'Libby?' Katherine frowned. 'Short for...?'

'Elizabeth.' She beamed again and when they just stood and openly stared she attempted conversation.

'We had a wonderful helicopter ride here. Your home is beautiful from the sky.'

Daniil watched as his mother fought not to step back from the warmth of Libby as she carried on with her observations. She dazzled and smiled when he was unable to and she filled the strained silence that usually ensued whenever he and his parents were together.

'Mind you, I should have worn flat shoes,' Libby continued. 'I'll be able to find my way in the dark—just follow the holes in the lawn—'

'Yes, well, guests are already arriving,' Katherine interrupted. 'Daniel, why don't you take Elizabeth to freshen up, but don't take too long. You've kept us waiting for quite long enough already.' A bell rang and Katherine looked around. 'Where the hell is Marcus?'

'He's taking our luggage up,' Daniil replied.

'Well, that's him gone for a week,' Katherine huffed, as she realised she might have to greet guests herself for a few moments. 'Why I offered to keep him on after retirement is beyond me. Go on, you two, get ready.'

Oh, she was completely awful, Libby thought as they went up the stairs. Her father only ever called her Elizabeth when he was telling her off.

They walked up the imposing staircase just as Marcus limped down, and Libby stiffened on the turn as a huge photograph came into sight. There, standing with the family, was a young Daniil, and it just about broke her heart to look at it. He was wearing a private school uniform and his eyes were hostile and it looked as if the effort of smiling for the camera might just be killing him.

Daniil refused to give it a glance.

'Daniel…' They both turned and there was Katherine,

who, Libby thought, looked a little like a fox terrier with her clipped hair and solid body. 'Charlotte just arrived.'

'And?'

'I'm just letting you know.'

He said nothing, just turned and carried on walking, but Katherine didn't leave things there. 'You'll be delivering a speech.'

'Of course.'

'It might be better if I skim through it...'

'No need,' he responded.

She had the tenacity of a terrier, too, Libby thought, as his mother followed them up the stairs.

'There's every need,' Katherine said. 'Daniel, our guests tonight, well, they're important...'

'Then, you'd better get back to them,' Daniil said, and taking Libby's arm he guided her down a corridor. Finally Katherine gave up and slunk back down the stairs.

'Tupa shmara,' Daniil cursed, as the bedroom door closed.

'I'm going to assume that you just said something terribly rude,' Libby said.

'Just the truth,' he responded, and looked around. Their cases sat closed, waiting to be unpacked, and he was grateful to Marcus for that.

To most the space would be inviting. The room was light and airy, the panelled walls were cream and offset by the dark wooden floor and door. The bay windows offered magnificent views of the estate and the furnishings, though antique, were peppered with modern touches. Daniil could well recall lying on the vast bed, watching television and not understanding more than a few words.

'It's beautiful,' Libby said, looking up at the plasterwork on the ceiling.

'If you like museums.' Daniil shrugged. She looked at the photos on the mantelpiece over a fireplace of Daniil holding a tennis racket and another of him sitting, scowling, on a horse. 'I was a poor replica of Daniel.'

'He'd have been a poor replica of you,' Libby said. 'I'm sure the guests would be terribly disappointed if I stepped into my sister's restaurant tonight and took over the kitchen. It would be like asking her to be my understudy—unthinkable! And we've got the same genes.'

She went over and wrapped her arms behind his neck as he looked around the bedroom he hated so much.

'Did you bring a lot of girls home?' Libby asked.

'I've never brought anyone here.'

'Till now,' Libby said, and she watched his eyes shutter, but she refused to be closed out and she stretched to reach his mouth, but he pulled back.

'Libby...' She could almost see the keep-out signs he held up.

'No.' She would not. She would enter at her own risk because that was where her heart led.

His jaw was like marble, his lips like ice, and one hand came up and went to unwrap her from his neck but she simply ignored him, pressing into those lips that she craved.

He was tense and reluctant yet she refused to be perturbed but then, just then, it was like cracking a safe, because she felt him give in to her mouth and he was pulling her closer, letting her in to a deep kiss.

Yes, she may not have his number but his mouth was familiar now, the way he led their kiss, the feeling that nothing and no one could reach them. His hands felt like silk, wrapping them tighter in the delicious cocoon they made.

'Not here,' he said, which was contrary to his actions, for his hand was pulling at the hem of her dress while at the same time pulling her in.

'Yes, here…' she breathed, disengaging her hand from around his neck and moving it down to between them, feeling the hard outline of him and running her palm over the swollen tip.

Yes, here, Daniil thought, for he was back in his old bedroom but he felt different this time, and his kiss was rough now, leading her to the bed. But suddenly there was a knock at the door and without waiting for a response it was opened.

Now she understood why he loathed people knocking at the door so much—it meant nothing, because, completely uninvited, in walked his father. Libby jumped back, embarrassed and shocked, ridiculously grateful that Daniil held one of her hands as the other smoothed her dress.

'*Se'bis,*' Daniil said.

'*Se'bis,*' Richard said, and a very flushed Libby frowned at the slight smirk on Daniil's face at his father's response. 'I've just been speaking with your mother about your speech,' Richard said. Daniil released Libby from his arms and she stood there, breathless, embarrassed and very, very angry at the intrusion, but she tried not to show it as Richard spoke on.

'I thought I might just take a quick look through it,' Richard said, but Daniil shook his head.

'There is no need for that.'

But his father was insistent. 'I just want to check that you've covered all bases.'

'I have.' Daniil refused to give in to him.

'Your mother's worried, Daniel. She's under a lot of

stress about tonight and isn't feeling well.' His hand moved to his chest and Libby thought the gesture was clearly meant to provoke a reaction.

'If she has chest pain then call an ambulance.' Daniil's response was calm and measured, unlike Richard's, whose hand balled in frustration as his son remained unmoved. 'Anyway—' Daniil shrugged '—there's nothing for you to see. I have my speech prepared here.' He tapped the side of his head. 'Now, if you will please excuse us, Libby and I would like to get ready. We'll be downstairs shortly.'

'Very well,' Richard said, but at the door he turned. Clearly, Libby thought, his father had to have the last word. 'But, Daniel, when you do come down, can you please lose the accent?'

They didn't get back to their kiss. Libby put on some make-up and tried to make sense of what she had just heard. It wasn't just an accent. Daniil's voice was one of the many beautiful things about him, and the thought they would censor that had tears sparkling in her eyes, which wasn't ideal when you were trying to put on eyeliner.

She simply didn't know what to say.

At first.

'Tupa shmara,' Libby hissed, and Daniil smiled.

'Nice try, wrong gender,' he said.

'Well, if we're having a Russian lesson, what does *se'bis* mean?' she asked, remembering the slight smirk when Daniil had greeted his father. Daniil laughed as he realised that Libby was far more perceptive than most.

'It means *get out,*' Daniil said. 'They always assumed I was saying it as a greeting when they came into my room. Soon enough they started to say it back to me! I took my victories where I could get them.'

'Ah, you can take the boy out of Russia…' Libby said, and even as they smiled, there was sadness there, for that, she realised, was exactly what his parents had done—they hadn't just taken him from his home, they had tried to erase his past, too.

'Your ambulance trips…' Libby said, and Daniil nodded.

'She would get chest pain or faint or whatever any time that she didn't get her way. It was always my fault, of course, but we had a lesson at school when I was four-teen about emergencies and first aid. The next time she collapsed I called an ambulance…'

'And?'

'I did the same the next time then the next time and the next…'

Libby looked into his cold grey eyes and could well picture him standing calm and detached as chaos sur-rounded him, but it didn't unsettle her. She knew, or was almost sure of, the warmth behind that guarded gaze.

'I can't be manipulated, Libby. Tears don't move me. Neither does drama.'

'What does, then?'

'Nothing.'

And therein lay a warning. This time, though, she was choosing not to heed it.

She didn't believe him.

'Let's do this,' he said, and they headed downstairs.

It was a supremely difficult evening.

Not for everybody else—after all Lindsey had seen to it that everything had been done to ensure that the celebration ran smoothly. The surroundings were sumptuous—the grand hall glittered, not just from the chandeliers but from the huge red pillar candles dotted around the room. The air was heavy with the scent of the deep red roses that were on each table, which, Katherine told anyone who listened, had been cultivated by their gardener just for this occasion. Yes, the caterers were fantastic, the band amazing; the whole kit and caboodle was brilliant.

'Your father did a good job,' Daniil commented, and then shook his head at a passing waiter as a drink was offered. Yes, everything was perfect—even Daniel Thomas, the wayward son, behaved beautifully and spoke with friends and family in a very schooled voice.

Didn't they get, Libby thought, *that when he had to think about what he was saying just to appease them, so much conversation was lost?*

No, she realised, they just cared about appearances. It wasn't Daniil that they wanted to know. He was merely a replacement for the Thomases' dead son.

'Daniel…' Libby bristled as a glossy brunette came over. Terribly glossy from her gleaming hair right to her blushing cheeks. 'It's been a long time.'

'Libby—' Daniil gave a tight smile '—this is Charlotte Stephenson. We were at school together. Charlotte's father was headmaster.'

'Still is,' Charlotte said, and then pointed across the hall. 'He's over there. You should go over and say hello.'

'Since when have I done as I should?' he replied.

Libby watched as Charlotte flounced off and she waited, waited for Daniil to explain, to tell her where Charlotte slotted in to his past, but, of course, he was supremely comfortable with silence, leaving Libby and her overactive imagination to fill in the gaps—of course, they'd been lovers.

Ah, and then they all paused for the wonderful speeches! Libby's throat was tight as Daniil walked to the front.

There was no fumbling in his pocket for his speech or hiding behind notes. He would speak, seemingly off the cuff, but Libby was quite sure of the hours of practice that must have taken place for him to be able to deliver this speech with apparent ease.

She glanced over at Katherine, who stood, eyes bulging and with a sheen of sweat on her upper lip. Richard, too, was tense, taking a hefty belt of his drink and then steeling himself as if preparing for bad news.

Would it be?

She looked at Daniil and for a moment wondered if he was about to wreak revenge for close to two decades of wrongs.

He'd thought about it.

For the first time in his life Daniil had the family stage, unmanaged. He looked at his parents and saw the tense warning in their eyes. He looked at his cousin George and his slight expectant smile, because wouldn't venting his spleen serve George's purpose well?

There was no need for the truth, though, Daniil thought, for there was no one here that he cared enough to explain it to.

And then his eyes met Libby's and possibly he would amend that thought soon.

For now he accepted her tight smile and the look that told him that whatever he chose to say was fine by her.

There was a slight heady relief that came when somebody accepted you, Daniil thought.

Whatever he might choose to do.

First, in perfect, clipped English, he thanked all the guests for coming, particularly those who had travelled from afar, and then he addressed his parents.

'Of course, the people who I really want to thank are the reason we are all here tonight.'

Libby heard the happy sigh trickle through the room and watched as both Katherine and Richard visibly relaxed. A smatter of applause paused Daniil's speech and she felt ashamed of herself, furious that she might have played any part in procuring this hell for him.

He went through his parents' marriage and spoke of their achievements, which were plenty, and the charities they supported, and then she watched Katherine's shoulders stiffen as Daniil brought the white elephant up to the front of the room.

'As you will all know, twenty years ago my parents suffered the devastating loss of their only child. For two years they were bereft but then, being the generous people that they are, they came to realise that they still had so much love to give.'

Libby wanted to stand up and clap. Not in applause. She wanted to stand and clap and call attention to herself. 'No, they didn't,' she wanted to say. 'They didn't want to deal with the death of their son so they simply did their best to get another one.'

Instead, though, she listened as he spoke on.

'As most of you will know, two years after their insufferable loss my parents brought me into their family. I was twelve years old at the time and—' he gave a wry smile '—far from easy, yet they opened their home to me and gave me opportunities that I could never have dreamed of.'

He spoke of the school they had sent him to, one where Richard was still on the board of directors.

'I see that Dr Stephenson is here tonight.' Daniil nodded to his old headmaster. 'You were right,' Daniil said, and it took everything he could to keep the malice from his eyes as he looked at man who had wielded his draconian power so mercilessly in an attempt to whip him into suitable shape. 'I had no idea just how lucky I was.'

Libby could feel the tension from her jaw right to her shoulders. Possibly she was the only person in the room who was reading between the lines, for Dr Stephenson was smiling as if he'd been thanked as Daniil continued.

'I know that without my parents' endless support and encouragement I would not be where I am today.'

Those present knew that financially Daniil was head and shoulders above everyone here and so, when he gave his parents the credit, there were oohs and aahs and applause from the crowd, and Katherine gave a small beatific smile and put her hand up to stop people, as if saying that she didn't deserve the praise.

She didn't, Libby thought savagely.

Yet Daniil saw it through.

He borrowed the line Libby had used on the day they had met, which he had at the time questioned, and said what an achievement forty years of marriage was. He wished them well for the future and said that their marriage was a shining example and one he could only hope to emulate.

As everyone raised their glasses, Libby was a few seconds behind. The expensive French champagne tasted like a dose of bitters on her tongue as Richard gave his first ever appreciative nod to his son.

Finally Daniil had toed the line.

I just sold my soul, Daniil thought as he returned to Libby's side.

But he had done it for a reason.

CHAPTER NINE

THE RED VELVET cake was cut and it looked amazing but sat like sand in her mouth as Daniil performed several duty dances.

Clearly she wasn't the only one who found the cake tasteless because the table she sat at became littered with discarded plates of half-eaten cake, but finally Daniil made his way over and now it was Libby he held in his arms.

'Your speech went down well,' she commented.

'The downside to that is they're now talking to me,' Daniil said. 'I preferred their silence.'

He glanced over Libby's shoulder and saw that his cousin was watching them. Libby had noticed him, too.

'Your cousin seems overly interested in you,' she observed.

'He's hoping I'll disgrace myself just to shore up his inheritance,' Daniil said. 'You know, sometimes I consider smarming up to my parents just for the dread it would cause him...'

'But you don't?'

'Nope,' Daniil said. 'I just amuse myself with the thought at times.' He looked down at Libby. His hands were on her waist and her spine was rigid and he missed the fluidity of her movements, the ease between them that they usually enjoyed.

'I'm sorry to have left you alone for so long.'

'It's fine.'

'We'll be out of here soon,' he said. He just wanted this night over so that he could speak with his father and find out a vital part of his past. He had no plans after that. His thought process had always stopped at the moment his father revealed the truth about the letters.

'We're not staying, then?' Libby checked, and then smiled. 'Or when you say out of here…'

She meant the bedroom, she meant a door between them and the rest of the world, and, for the first time ever, he realised that might be enough. He looked down into clear blue eyes and the thought of staying the night was appealing if it meant that they could be alone sooner.

'You've seen for yourself how my father had no compunction about knocking and not waiting to be asked in…'

'We could cure that annoying habit very easily,' Libby said into his ear.

'It didn't work this evening.'

'I wasn't naked and on top of you then,' Libby said, and Daniil found himself smiling at the thought of his father's hasty retreat if he found them in such a compromising position.

'You wouldn't duck under the covers, would you?'

'Of course not,' she said. 'I'd ask him to pour me a glass of water. He'd never not knock again.'

'What are you doing?' Daniil asked, as she smiled and gave a small wave to someone over his shoulder.

'I'm annoying George for you,' she said. 'I just smiled at your mother.'

Here at the family home, when he had never thought there could be, there was the first glimpse of ease. With Libby, there was a sense of togetherness—nothing and no one could touch them.

'What are your family functions like?' Daniil asked.

'Catered for by my sister, micromanaged by my father...'

'And your mother?' Daniil asked, because she rarely mentioned her.

'Frowned on by her.' Libby's response was resigned. 'I don't think she's ever been truly happy. She simply doesn't know how to enjoy the moment.'

And that was exactly what they did.

Right now, in the midst of so much history, a sliver of pleasure was found—the beat of the music, the feel of each other.

Was this what a relationship made possible? Daniil pondered.

A hellish visit made bearable simply by having her there.

Always there was the next thing to aim for, the race to be run, but right now, in a place that held no happy memories, where he had least expected to find it, he started to glimpse a future, a constant that could remain.

The dance had turned into one of pleasure, an unexpected treasure that he had never expected to find this night, though it unnerved Daniil, rather than bought comfort, for he knew better than to get used to such a thing.

Nothing lasted—that much had been proved long ago.

As the music shifted he released her from his arms and Libby excused herself to visit the ladies' room. Daniil went and got another glass of sparkling water—he was very deliberately not drinking tonight.

He stiffened as George came over to him—he was all smiles as he congratulated Daniil on his speech.

'Very nicely said.' George gave a nod of approval that Daniil did not need but, because he *had* sold his soul tonight, just to find out about the letters, he seemingly accepted the praise and shook his cousin's hand.

'It's true what you said about a forty-year marriage being an achievement…' George sighed. 'I doubt it will ever happen to either of us.'

'Yes, I heard about your divorce,' Daniil said. He really was on his best behaviour tonight, for he omitted to mention that this divorce would be George's third.

'Yes, the cow is taking me for all I haven't got,' George hissed. 'The last two saw to that. Relationships are bloody hard work if you ask me.'

Daniil hadn't.

'So how long have you been with Libby?' George asked. 'She seems like a very lovely lady.'

'She is.'

'How did you meet?'

'We…' Daniil started, and then he realised there was no reason to lie. 'We met through Libby's father. He organised tonight.'

'So you only got together recently, then?'

Daniil nodded.

'I thought as much.'

'Excuse me?' Daniil checked.

'She still seems happy,' George said, and walked off.

Daniil's jaw gritted but he told himself to ignore what had just been said. As he went to walk away it was straight into Charlotte, who was standing, talking with his mother and her father.

'For old times' sake?' Charlotte said.

It was a duty dance or make a small scene, Daniil knew, so he held his ex in loose hands and, had Libby not been here tonight, she'd have sufficed.

Charlotte didn't do it for him now.

'My father's looking very displeased,' Charlotte whispered, and twelve years or so ago that would have turned him on.

Hell, a few weeks ago it might have been enough for Daniil to make his way to her room later tonight for the simple pleasure of screwing her under her father's nose.

'I'm coming down to London next week,' Charlotte purred.

'I'll be away on business.'

'I'll be there again next month.'

And he knew then he'd changed because next month was an eternity in the relationship stakes for him and yet he was starting to envision the weeks with Libby—imagining that, weeks from now, months from now, years from now, they two might remain. Yes, Charlotte was like the cake, perfect to look at yet something was lacking. There was no temptation to taste now.

'Why don't you give me your number?' Charlotte asked. 'I tried calling a while back but your receptionist wouldn't put me through. If I had your—'

'I don't give it out to just anyone,' Daniil interrupted.

'I'm not just anyone.'

And he looked into eyes that were playing the game he had played for so long, yet he was over it now.

'Oh, but you are.'

Yes, he was the bastard she told him he was, and as Libby returned to the grand hall it was to the sight of Charlotte walking rapidly away from his arms.

No, Libby wasn't secure enough not to notice or care.

The evening was winding down and Daniil just wanted to get out of this toxic place but he still hadn't spoken with his father and as Richard came over, he decided to deal with that now.

'We're going riding in the morning,' Richard said. 'It will be an early start and then back here for breakfast…'

'Not for me,' Daniil said. 'We need to head off before nine. I was wondering if I could have a word, though.'

'Now really isn't the best time.'

Libby was by his side, watching the terse exchange, feeling Daniil's hand tighten around her fingers.

'It will only take a few moments.'

Richard gave a very stiff nod and as he walked off Daniil went to follow him. Given he was holding her hand, Libby walked with them, but as they reached the entrance hall Daniil seemed to remember she was there and let go.

'I need to speak with my father.'

'I could come with you.'

He shot her a look that told her she had overstepped the mark and she didn't know her place here.

'Go to sleep. I'll be up later.'

'Sleep?' Libby said. 'People are still dancing, the party hasn't finished…'

'It has for us.' Already he had gone and she stood there, trying to comprehend such a dismissal. She gave a wide, though incredulous smile as Marcus the butler came over.

'I think I've just been sent to bed.' Libby shook her head in bewilderment. One moment they had been dancing and together, the next she had been packed off to bed.

Daniil stood there as Libby flounced up the stairs and then followed his father into the dark bowels of the house—Richard's study. As they walked in and his father took a seat at his desk Daniil remembered standing here, handing over his report cards. But he wasn't a teenager now and he stood taller than the man who had so badly bullied him.

'I can guess what you're here for,' Richard said. 'Your mother and I have spoken at length about the inheritance—'

'I am not here about your estate,' Daniil interrupted, and he watched his father press his lips together as his son's public school voice fell away and Daniil stood, menacing, challenging and defiant. 'What you do there is your business. I've never had an interest in your money.'

Air whistled out of Richard's nostrils in frustration. One of the many things that irked him was that Daniil could buy and sell him several times over.

'The letters.' Daniil had known exactly what he planned to say, but in the courtroom of his father's study for a moment he felt as if he was back to being a teenager and the words did not flow. 'I want to know—'

'Ah, yes.' Richard went into his desk. 'A deal's a deal. Though there was only one.'

Daniil frowned as his father took out an envelope. He did everything not to display need but his hand was shaking as he took it from his father. The writing was in English but it had been written by a Russian, Daniil could tell that from the curve of the letters and the numbers.

It must be from Roman!

He wanted to rip it open there and then but he just stared at it, looking at the stamps from home and the faded writing and trying to read the postmark as hope started to rise in his chest—finally he had contact with his twin.

'When did this come?' Daniil asked.

'Oh, it would be five or six years ago now.'

'What?' Daniil growled, glad he had asked his father about the letter now, rather than earlier in the evening. If they'd had this exchange then, the only speech he would have been capable of delivering would have been his statement to the police when they arrested him, such was the temptation to lash out.

Instead, he contained it.

He still had questions.

'Why didn't you give me this at the time?' Daniil asked.

'We didn't want you raking up the past.'

'It's *my* past,' he said. 'You can't take that from me. God knows, you've tried, though.' A little of his temper unleashed. 'Why did you give it to me now?'

'I told Lindsey it might persuade you to come.'

Did Libby know?

It was irrelevant, Daniil knew. This letter had lain hidden in a desk for years. A few weeks made no difference; he just wasn't thinking logically now.

He wanted out.

'Will you answer one question?' Daniil asked, and Richard gave a nod. 'The letters I gave you to post to my brother—were they ever sent? I'd really appreciate the truth.'

Perhaps Richard knew it might well be the last time they came face-to-face, perhaps he accepted this man would never be his son because he tapped in the final nail.

'They weren't sent.'

'Can I ask why?'

'All the advice we got was that if you were to success-fully integrate...'

'No,' Daniil said. 'You disposed of the advice you were given and sought puppets who would tell you what you wanted to hear.'

'You'd be on the streets without us, Daniel, or locked up. The temper you had—'

'Richard,' Daniil interrupted. He would never go through the farce of calling him Father again. *'Otyebis ot menya.'*

He told his father to get the hell away from him, though rather less politely than that, and then he told him, in Russian, to *stay* the hell away.

He could not stand to be in a room with him a moment longer. He wanted the door between himself and his family that Libby had alluded to, their privacy, but as he walked to the stairs, unable to resist, he tore open the letter. All he could see was that it wasn't from Roman but Sev.

It said that he was in London for one day and could they meet?

The letter had been sent five years ago!

He saw the portrait of his so-called family on the turn of the stairs and felt like ripping the picture off the wall and putting his foot through it, or calling his pilot and leaving now, but then he remembered he'd told Libby to get some sleep and tearing her from her bed in some angry display didn't appeal.

Instead, he walked out onto a balcony and watched the partygoers leave, staring out into the black countryside as he had done so many times growing up, and finally he took out the letter and read it properly.

Hey, *shishka*!

Daniil's jaw still clenched when he read that name but there was a smile, too, at the memory and he read on painfully.

I met a woman who wanted me because I was Russian; she was hung up on a guy she once slept with—Daniel Thomas.

That didn't sound very Russian to me and so I looked him up.

You've done well.

I am going to be in America for a month making some rich man richer but I will be in London on the twelfth of November. I don't know where to suggest we meet, all I know there is a palace? Midday?

I hope my writing to you doesn't cause you embarrassment.

Sev

There was nothing about Roman, or Nikolai, no hint about their lives, and he ached to know something, anything about the past he had been forced to leave behind.

He was, though, five years too late to find out.

He looked out at the sky that was black to match his mood.

There were no stars.

Despite the warmth of the day it was now one of those crisp nights that heralded the end of summer.

The end of them?

In the same selfish way that Daniil had wanted Libby here tonight he wanted to head back to his bedroom. He wanted it to be just the two of them and the uncomplicated world that was there, but he was more than aware of his own dark mood.

George's comment was like a worm in his ear. He tried to shrug off his cousin's words—he knew just how poisonous he could be—and yet, as always, there was an element of truth.

How long would Libby be happy for?

How much would he put her through before that perpetual smile disappeared from her face for good?

He had no experience with relationships, no hook to hang hope on, nothing to recall. There were vivid memories of yesteryear, and look how that had worked out.

Roman had made no effort to contact him.

Neither had Nikolai.

One letter five years ago from Sev was all he had from his past.

It wasn't much to go on. It didn't instil the necessary confidence it would take to tell her the hollow disappointment he felt tonight.

She was surely better out of it.

CHAPTER TEN

LIBBY WASN'T SLEEPING.

As she stepped into Daniil's old bedroom it would seem that it wasn't just helicopters that Libby was averse to because she had the strange feeling again of the floor coming up to meet her. She sat, a touch dizzy, on the bed and wondered if maybe she'd eaten something that hadn't agreed with her.

Or drunk something, perhaps?'

But that didn't work because even the glass of champagne she'd taken to toast his parents had tasted bitter and she'd struggled to swallow a sip down.

She was overtired, Libby decided.

Of course she was. After all, she'd been busy with her new business and rushing around with the banks and open nights and things.

That made no sense, either, because what might seem an exhausting few weeks to some felt like a holiday to Libby—she was used to being up at six and warming up, ready to start her first dance class at eight. Rehearsals had commenced at ten, then there had been matinee and evening productions, and, even if she'd been playing the smallest of roles, it had still been well after midnight before she'd got into bed. And as well as all that she'd had to rehearse for roles she'd been understudying.

So, no, despite feeling drained, there was no real reason to be tired, or was she simply in turmoil from falling head over heels for a man who had warned her from the get-go not to get too attached?

Perhaps he should have been more specific; perhaps he should have also told her not to go and do something as foolish as to get pregnant!

Libby voiced it for the first time in her head as she lay there, staring up at the intricate plasterwork on the ceiling, and then she chided herself for her complete overreaction.

She wasn't even late.

Well, barely.

Amenorrhea was the dancer's curse, Libby told herself.

It just didn't ring true tonight.

She jumped when she heard a knock at the door, knowing Daniil would never knock and wondering if Richard or Katherine was about to burst in.

There was another knock on the door.

'Come in,' Libby said, and as the door opened she saw that it was Marcus with a tray. She let out a sigh of relief.

'I thought you might like some tea.'

'I would.' Libby smiled. 'That's very kind of you.'

There wasn't just tea, there were biscuits and a slice of cake, too, as well as a jug of iced water. It was rather nice to have supplies while she was shut away!

'Is Daniil still speaking with his father?'

'I'm not sure,' Marcus said, as he poured her tea, and then he gave a tight smile that spoke volumes. 'I expect they shan't be too long.'

'Is it always this tense when Daniil is home?' Libby asked, as she took her cup. Oh, she knew she was talking out of turn but she simply couldn't help herself. She expected to be chastised or for some vague, polite, dismissive answer but the cup rattled in the saucer as Marcus, far more directly than Libby was expecting, responded.

'It's *always* this tense.'

She looked up at Marcus's kind lined face, surprised at his indiscretion, wondering if he would retract or attempt to cover up what he'd said. She saw that he was looking directly at her, almost inviting her to speak.

'And yet you're staying on after your retirement?'

'Oh, no,' Marcus replied. 'Sometimes we just say things to appease, though, of course, Daniil has never mastered that art.' He looked around the room. 'I remember the day he arrived here. I was just about to hand in my notice—the last thing I needed was another spoiled preteen telling me what to do—but then he arrived and...' He shook his head. 'Well, there was so much damage...'

Libby swallowed and then opened her mouth to speak. It hurt to hear Daniil described as that but her protest died on her lips as Marcus carried on talking. 'Far too much damage to leave a child to deal with, especially one who spoke no English.'

It was the biggest insight she had ever had.

'So you stayed?'

'Yes, I chose to stay for a few weeks to ease him in and that turned into a few months, then years. I decided to leave when Daniil started university.'

'But you didn't?'

'A new cook started.' Marcus smiled and he glanced at the tray he had brought up and saw that the cake was untouched. 'Shirley. You have no idea how many times she tried to get that cake right…' He didn't elaborate. 'Of course, we've never told the Thomases about us—they'd have had us moved to couples accommodation on half the wage.'

'Why are you telling me this?' Libby was as direct as ever with her questions.

'You asked,' Marcus said. 'That's very rare around here. Anyway, suffice it to say, in a few weeks' time Shirley and I shall retire, and it can't come a moment too soon.'

He said no more than that, just gave a smile and wished her goodnight.

After he had gone Libby undressed and climbed into the vast bed and flicked out the side lights. Noise filtered through and she longed for the thick double-glazed windows of her little flat, which kept the sound of the buses and cars out. Here the windows were old and allowed her to listen to the guests leaving and the crunch of cars on gravel and the sound of helicopters lifting into the sky and even, at one point, Sir Richard's voice, laughing at something someone had said and then wishing them a safe journey home.

She heard George guffaw at something and, no, her straining ears told her that Daniil wasn't locked in conversation with them.

And she lay there, alone, and as it edged towards three in the morning she wondered if he had gone already. She didn't know if he'd simply upped and left. Maybe he'd forgotten she was there, like some discarded bag on a train that he'd suddenly recall at midday tomorrow, and make a few half-hearted calls to retrieve.

She remembered only too well how cautious she had been when she had accepted his invitation to dinner that

first night. Then she had ensured that she'd had enough
money in her purse to offer an escape route.

Tonight she had none.

All she could do was wonder why he would prefer to
be alone than with her.

If he *was* alone.

Doubts were as long and black as the shadows that
were cast in the room.

Fear that she could be pregnant did not foster restful
sleep. There was a need to accelerate things, to know exactly what she was dealing with, so her eyes were wide-
open when, well after four, the door opened and Daniil
came in.

'Where were you?' she said, as she listened to him
undress.

'I've never answered that question in my life and I
don't intend to start now.'

'So I'm supposed to just lie here, waiting…'

'I never asked you to wait up for me.'

It disconcerted him that she had. Daniil had assumed
that Libby would have been asleep long ago. He was used
to operating on his own hours and he wasn't used to ac-
counting for his time.

'I hope she was worth it.' Libby closed her eyes in
regret as soon as that sentence was out. It sounded jealous, suspicious, needy, but, hell, four hours waiting for
the master to return and that was exactly how she felt.
'Were you with Charlotte?'

'Grow up!' Daniil said. 'Do you really think I've spent
the past few hours flirting with some ghost from my
past? Making out with Dr Stephenson's daughter to get
my kicks…?' His voice trailed off and she listened to
him undress.

'Is that what you used to do?' Libby asked. 'Was she a part of your rebellion?'

'Yep.' Daniil's response was blithe.

'Any other ex-lovers here tonight?' she asked, as she lay there bristling.

'Many,' Daniil answered. 'The village pub closes at eleven—which was far too early to come back to this hellhole.' He climbed into bed and she could feel the cool come in under the sheets and it dawned on her that he had spent all that time outside.

Rather than be here with her.

'All I know is…' Libby started, but didn't finish.

'All you know is what?' he said, pushing her to complete whatever it was she had been about to say.

'Nothing,' she admitted. 'I have no idea where we are or where we're going…' She turned and looked at him. He was lying on his back, staring up at the ceiling, with his hands behind his head, and though sharing a bed he might just as well have been in another room.

'Nowhere,' Daniil said. 'I told you the night we met— we're going nowhere.'

'Bastard.'

'You have no idea the bastard I can be, Libby.'

'I'm starting to find out,' she said. 'I don't understand what's happened. I know that something has, but rather than tell me you'd leave me lying here, wondering where the hell you were.'

'I was out on the balcony, if you *must* know.'

'I *want* to know.'

She was demanding. It was all or nothing with Libby— that was how she lived her life. With Daniil she felt she was supposed to hold back, to restrain herself, to feign nonchalance, but that wasn't who she was.

'Did you know anything about a letter for me?'

'Yes, about your inheritance, I think…' Libby was vague.

'Actually, no, it was a letter to me.'

'Well, how would I know that?' she said.

'Go to sleep,' he said.

'If only it were that easy. I'm sorry if I'm not laid-back enough for you. I apologise if I can't sleep the sleep of the dead when I've no idea where you are.'

No one had ever waited up for him.

Occasionally Marcus had let him in if he'd had arrived home late minus his keys. That was the sum of concern in this place.

He recalled one Christmas Eve, when he'd been about seventeen, and a night at the local pub had seemed more palatable than a night spent with his parents, George and Dr Stephenson and family.

He'd been unable to get a taxi from the village and had rather foolishly decided to take the long walk home in the snow. He hadn't counted on the lack of landmarks, or that a few drinks on a stomach of dread might make for a difficult journey. He had given in and holed up in a barn, waking to a weak silvery sunrise before tackling the last mile home.

Marcus had let him in and, following voices, Daniil had walked into the drawing room to see his parents opening their presents, along with George.

They had all turned as he had stepped in, his black hair white with snow, his clothes damp from a night sleeping out, but what had truly frozen out that Christmas morning had been his mother's slight shrug. 'Oh!' she had said. 'We thought you were still in bed.'

Daniil looked over to where Libby lay. He knew that his anger was misplaced.

'I thought you would be asleep.'

'Well, I wasn't.'

'I know that now.'

He'd entered the room determined to stay away but now he rolled towards her, his cold mouth seeking hers, his hands everywhere, but she slapped them off.

'You'd rather screw me than talk to me.'

'Tonight, yes.'

'Well, tough,' she said. 'You can't ignore me for half the night and then expect peak performance...'

He rolled away from her and she lay regretting her stance and yet refusing to relent.

She lay facing away from him perhaps as lonely and scared as Daniil had been all those years ago in this very room. After all, her problem was the same as his had been—it was hard to accept that you weren't really wanted.

CHAPTER ELEVEN

LIBBY MUST HAVE drifted off to sleep because she woke to the sound of Daniil in the shower and the recollection of their row.

Maybe she had been too harsh. Libby knew from the little he had told her that coming back here would prove hard but, hell, she was tired of numbing their issues with sex.

She watched as he walked out of the en suite, still sulking.

He dried himself and she looked at his beautiful, toned, sensual body and really she should give herself a gold star for managing to say no to that last night.

She was tired of the roller-coaster ride, though.

For the best part of a year she had lived on one, courtesy of her fading career. Having stepped off that one, she had promptly climbed into a carriage named Daniil, yet she had forgotten to strap herself in.

It was time to rectify that.

'Are we going down for breakfast?' she asked, as her stomach declared it would like some.

'No,' Daniil said.

'Well, thanks for keeping me informed.'

She headed into the en suite and looked at her pale

complexion and white lips and prayed her pallor was down to the fact she was getting her period.

Her breasts certainly felt as if she was, Libby thought as she showered and felt them swollen and sensitive beneath her fingers.

She simply couldn't be pregnant.

Apart from the fact that it would mean the father was possibly London's most notorious rake, there was a little thing called the Libby Tennent School of Dance to consider. It was the summation of her life's work and her entire future. The dance school had felt for a while like a last resort but it was where all her hope resided now.

Yes, maybe her anger last night and this morning was a touch illogical and misdirected, yet that was how she felt—*illogical* and *misdirected* were apt words to describe her behaviour since Daniil had come into her life.

She stepped out of the shower and looked into the mirror, barely turning as Daniil, dressed in black jeans and a black crew-neck, came and stood behind her.

Apart from naked, she had never seen him out of a suit and she was angry that he looked better, if possible. Unshaven, scowling, his expression matched her mood.

'You didn't knock.'

'You know how I feel about knocking,' he said. 'What's wrong, Libby?' He gave a hollow laugh at his own question. 'Aside from me not coming back last night, but we were fine until then.'

'No,' Libby corrected. 'We weren't.'

She was naked but she never felt that with him and unabashed she turned and faced him.

'Has there been anyone else since me?'

He blinked at her forthright question and, guessing this was still about Charlotte, he just shrugged. There was no need to be evasive or to think so he simply answered, 'No.'

'So we've been seeing each other for a month?'

'I don't think it's been a month.'

Now he was being evasive.

'Yes.' Libby nodded and then proceeded to tick off their encounters on her fingers. 'It has been—we had dinner and then the next week I came by your office and then the next week you came by my studio and then the next week here we are.'

'And tonight I am going overseas on business for a few nights,' Daniil said. He didn't like a numbers game; he didn't want it confirmed but they had been together a month. 'I don't get your point.'

'Then, I'll explain it.'

She had nothing to lose, not even her pride—that had long since gone out of the window where Daniil was concerned. She was tired of things being one-sided, tired of expending emotion on a man who was so reluctant to give it back.

'I don't have your phone number,' she said. 'Your apartment is like Fort Knox and your receptionist is so intimidating I can't imagine myself popping in...'

'I don't get where you're going with this.'

'Then, listen,' Libby said. 'I want flowers, I want conversation, I want phone calls and texts and presents...' He went to open his mouth but she got there first. 'And before you accuse me of demanding expensive gifts, that's not what I mean. I'm tired of living on a knife edge. It's not all about whether you want to see me again, Daniil. It's about whether or not I want to see you, too, and if you can't be bothered to pick up your phone and ask about my day then I don't want you to be a part of it anymore.'

She was through with prolonging endings. If they were over, if he couldn't offer more than a weekly visit, then they were done.

'Is that it?' he said.

'That's it,' she replied, and brushed past him to the bedroom, where she opened the overnight bag that she had packed with such hope and, of course, that wasn't quite it.

'Don't think you can return from your business trip and pick up where we left off.'

'Why would I want to pick up where we left off? From what I recall, last night wasn't exactly—'

'It's not all about sex.'

'Actually, for me, it is.'

'Then, you *really* did bring the wrong date last night.'

'I don't like pushy—'

'Same answer,' Libby responded. 'You're with the wrong person, then. I'm affectionate, I'm demonstrative, that's who I am. If you want some nonchalant lover then you're with the wrong woman. I'm not going to pretend I don't care just because that's what you'd prefer.'

'Have you finished?'

'Yes.'

She had.

Libby was as lovely with his parents as she had been on arrival and as Marcus came from the helicopter where he had deposited their luggage she gave him a fond hug.

Yet as the helicopter lifted off there was no touching hands this time. Instead, she closed her eyes and dozed for the journey home.

Even on the car ride back to her flat she was silent.

'When I get back maybe we could…' Daniil started, but she was already climbing out of the car.

She could see the curtain flickering and knew Rachel would be waiting for an update and would scold her for not playing it cool. But where Daniil was concerned there was no such thing as lukewarm; there was no question now of sitting on the fence and waiting to see what his next move would be.

Libby delivered her ultimatum.

'I don't do well with maybes so if you leave it till then don't bother calling—it will be too late,' she said. 'I mean it.'

His car didn't sit idling until she was safely inside.

And neither did Libby turn and wave.

He was in or out and so was she.

She just hoped that some time this century her heart would catch up with that fact.

To her shame, that night Libby took her phone to her bed *and* plugged it into its charger.

Just in case.

But she woke to no calls or texts and no flowers, either.

He's on a business trip, she reminded herself, though it was a poor excuse because he could probably have a koala bear delivered to her if he so chose.

And on Tuesday, again nothing.

Even her period refused to make itself known. That evening, Libby came in the door and tried to pretend to Rachel that she wasn't scanning the hall, kitchen and lounge for flowers and she asked, oh, so casually, 'Any phone calls?'

'Only your parents call you on the landline. I warned you…'

'He might still be flying…'

'Oh, so his personal pilot would have told him to turn

his phone off? You shouldn't have pushed so hard,' Rachel said, because Libby had told her some, if not all, about the weekend she and Daniil had shared.

'Why not?' Libby said. 'I'd be being ignored now whatever I'd said. At least this way I know he's not interested.'

On Wednesday she played good toes, naughty toes with a group of very wriggly four-year-olds and listened to the sound of babies crying in her tiny waiting room.

She couldn't possibly be pregnant, Libby thought as she pointed her toes down.

'Good toes,' she said, deciding that she was lovesick, that was all.

'Very, very naughty toes,' Libby said, wondering why the hell she'd been foolish enough to do it without protection.

Eight little girls blinked at the deviation from the script and the sound of their ballet teacher's slightly strange laughter.

'Good toes,' Libby said, because, hell, he hadn't come inside her.

But they were soon back to naughty toes and dark thoughts that maybe he was so potent that his sperm would be the same, brutally tapping away at her poor egg just as he had at her heart.

As she waited for her older students to arrive Libby went into her locker and looked at the pregnancy test kit she had bought but hadn't had the courage to use.

She was scared to find out.

There was the temporary distraction of a young adult class later that evening. For now it consisted of three— Sonia, a girl called Oonagh and a young man called Henry, who had so much talent it both thrilled and scared her to have a hand in moulding it. But her fears caught up with her as she made her way home.

A broken heart she could deal with.

Possibly, an unexpected pregnancy, too.

It was Daniil Zverev who had her stomach somersaulting.

He was the most remote, distant man she had ever met.

The antithesis of her.

A man who had told her from the very start he didn't get close to anyone, and now with every day that passed it was more and more likely he was going to be the father of her child.

'You look like death,' Rachel said, as she came in the door. 'Your father called…'

'I know,' Libby said. 'I just spoke to him.'

Dr Stephenson was retiring and had asked Lindsey if he could organise the party, and he also wondered if Libby might consider travelling to Oxford to discuss it.

'He was most impressed,' Lindsey had said.

'I'm not meeting with him, Dad.'

'You're a point of contact.'

'No,' Libby had said. 'I'm not.'

The last thing she wanted now was a trip to Oxford and a trip down memory lane when it looked as if the next few months would be taken up getting over Daniil.

Getting bigger by him.

Libby looked over at Rachel, wondering if she should tell her friend just what was on her mind.

Rachel would be brilliant; Libby knew that. She'd dash off to the chemist and in half an hour or so…

She'd know.

Maybe she already did.

'You didn't ask if there had been any phone calls or deliveries,' Rachel observed.

'You'd have told me if there had been,' Libby sighed. 'Please, don't say you warned me.'

'I shan't.'

'Maybe I should have done what you said and—'

'No,' Rachel interrupted. 'If you had, then he'd have been in for a very rude shock a few weeks or months down the line. You're right, it's better to be yourself from the start.'

'Even if that self is pushy and demanding?' Libby checked.

'Yep, I'm proud of you for standing firm.'

'You know, he warned me not to go falling in love, I should have—' She never got to finish. Instead, she jumped as the one moment she wasn't looking at her phone it bleeped with a text.

'Oh!' Libby let out a shout of joy when she read it. 'It's from Daniil.'

'What does he say?' Rachel checked as Libby started tapping away.

Hi. Daniil.

'That's it?' Rachel checked, and then jumped up and tried to wrestle the phone from her friend but was already too late—Libby's response had been sent.

Hearts, flowers, kisses, she had used every emoticon at her disposal and Rachel was appalled.

'I thought you were proud of me for being myself,' Libby said, as she chewed on her nails. She knew her response had been over the top and wondered if it was possible to retrieve a text.

Even if it was possible, it was way too late for that, she thought as she saw the little tick beside her message that meant it had been read. 'I should have just said hi.'

'You should have waited two hours before saying hi,' Rachel reprimanded.

'I know, I just—'

Then it rang.

'Daniil!' Libby exclaimed.

He smiled at the obvious delight in her voice and could compare it to nothing else—it was unchecked, without agenda and simply her.

'I missed you,' Libby said, and Rachel cringed.

'I miss you, too,' he admitted. 'And I'm ringing to tell you that I lied.'

'I'm quite sure you did,' she said, waving to Rachel as she headed into her bedroom. 'About what? Charlotte?'

Daniil laughed at the edge to her voice.

'I don't lie about things that don't matter. I'm not away on business, I'm in Russia.'

'Oh.'

'I'm trying to find out what happened to the others.'

'Have you had any luck?'

'Not really,' he said, and then with that hopefully out of the way he changed the subject. 'How are you?'

Libby hesitated. She wanted to tell him she was floating on air just to hear from him, she wanted to tell him that her period was AWOL and she had never been more scared in her life, but somehow she managed to find the off switch.

'Busy,' she said. 'The classes are filling up.'

'That's good.'

'Why did you call?' she asked.

'I didn't like how we left things. I was a bastard the other night…'

'I know that you were,' she said.

'I didn't mean to be. I really thought you would be asleep.'

'I know that now,' she said. 'So what's this letter your father gave you?'

'Do we have to talk about it?' Daniil asked.

'No,' Libby said, but it was like being told not to push a button or knowing that her parents were out and her Christmas presents were in the wardrobe. 'Yes.'

'You have no patience.'

'Not a scrap.'

'Okay, I got a letter from Sev.'

'One of your friends from the orphanage?'

'Yes, he must have found my parents' address and sent it to them. He was asking to meet me outside Buckingham Palace. I guess it was the only place he had heard of in London but they never gave it to me till that night. My father said they didn't want to rake up the past.'

'How long ago was it sent?'

'Five years ago.'

'What does it say?'

'Just that.'

'Tell me.'

Daniil sighed and picked up the letter he had just been looking at.

'He says, "Hey, *shishka*."'

'*Shishka?*'

'It's slang for big shot. They started to call me that when they found out that I was going to be adopted.'

'What else does it say?'

Daniil wasn't sure he should translate the next part verbatim but he did so and read it out loud, telling her about the woman Sev had nearly slept with, and about meeting outside Buckingham palace at midday in November.

'What else?'

'Nothing,' Daniil said. 'Well, he says that he hopes his writing wouldn't embarrass me.'

'Why would his writing embarrass you?' she asked.

'He would think I wanted nothing to do with him.'

'At least it's something to work on,' Libby said, but he disagreed.

'There's nothing—no contact address in the letter, no surname. There's no more information than that. We didn't do much schooling in letter writing.'

Daniil had scanned every part of his memory to try to recall the surnames of Sev and Nikolai. They had never used or needed them where they had lived.

'Have you been to the orphanage?'

'It's a school now,' he said, 'but I've been asking around. Sergio, he was the maintenance man, has since died but I spoke to his wife this afternoon. Sev got a scholarship to a good school and Nikolai left when he was fourteen.'

'For where?'

'He ran away,' Daniil said and was quiet for a moment. 'He drowned.'

'Oh, no,' Libby wailed but Daniil carried on speaking in his low voice.

Last night he had cried.

'Katya—she was the cook—apparently left to follow her daughter, Anya, to St Petersburg.'

'Roman?'

'Nothing. I'm trying to find out if he did his military service but apart from that there are no more leads.'

'Well, November is just a couple of months away. Why don't you try to meet Sev then?'

'I'm five years late,' Daniil pointed out.

'Well, it's still worth a try. I know if I'd written that letter that I'd be there every year, like some sad old thing, holding a rose…'

She made him smile.

'Can we start again?' Daniil said.

'Can we?' she asked, wishing it were that easy.

'I thought we might go out on a date, a proper date. I've bought tickets for *Firebird*. I could pick you up and go out to dinner…'

Libby lay on her bed in silence. She hadn't watched a ballet production since she had made the decision to end her career and she didn't know if she was ready to go and see beauty unfold and not be in it. She knew she would be aching to take part and yet he really was making an effort to give them a new start.

'I don't know…' she said, but Daniil spoke over her doubt, quoting *A Winter's Journey* by Polonsky, on which the ballet was based.

'"And in my dreams I see myself on a wolf's back
Riding along a forest path
To do battle with a sorcerer-tsar
In that land where a princess sits under lock and key,
Pining behind massive walls.
There gardens surround a palace all of glass,
There Firebirds sing by night
And peck at golden fruit."'

His voice made her shiver.

'Sev used to read to us at night,' Daniil said and thought back to that time. 'Come and see a nice wolf for once.'

'Is there such a thing?'

'Maybe it's time to find out.'

After the call ended Libby wondered if she'd done the right thing in agreeing to go.

It had to be the right thing, she decided, swinging her legs off the bed and standing up.

A date.

A proper one.

Their first.

'Well?' Rachel said, when she came out of the bedroom.

'He's taking me to see *Firebird* on Saturday.'

'That was thoughtful of him.' Rachel rolled her eyes. 'What an insensitive jerk.'

'He doesn't know.'

'Then tell him what you told me just a couple of weeks ago, that you're dreading going to see a full production.'

'That was a couple of weeks ago,' Libby said.

'You're sure?'

Libby nodded and headed over to the calendar that they kept on the fridge so that they would loosely know each other's comings and goings.

'Firebird,' Libby wrote boldly, even if she felt sick at the thought of it, but then again she felt sick all the time anyway…

She flicked the calendar back and remembered the last week she'd spent with the company, blaming her up-and-down mood and tears on the time of the month.

She was going on her *first* date with Daniil and there was no getting away from it now—she was five days late.

Libby stepped away from the calendar as if closing the stable door.

The horse might already have bolted.

CHAPTER TWELVE

LIBBY DRESSED IN a simple black dress and shoes and took extra care with her make-up and this time, as she waited for Daniil to arrive, she didn't sit on the window ledge, looking out for him.

It had nothing to do with playing it cool, she simply couldn't relax.

'When did he get back from his business trip?'

'I'm not sure,' Libby said.

There had been one text and one phone call in total. It had taken a herculean effort not to call him back each night, not to text and ask when he would be home, or for confirmation of times for tonight.

No flowers again, no cyber displays of affection.

Still, she lived in a state of suspension, courtesy of the man who was taking her out tonight.

'I am looking forward to it,' she said to Rachel. 'It's just…'

'I know.'

'I'll probably enjoy it once I'm there,' she said, though it was more to convince herself. She wanted to see Daniil; tonight was important for so many reasons. It was their first date, a new start for both of them.

It wasn't just seeing *Firebird* that weighed heavily on

her mind, though, and she excused herself for the second time in an hour and fled to the bathroom. She was just about over convincing herself it was nerves that accounted for the constant feeling of nausea.

How could she tell him? she wondered.

She couldn't, she decided, even though she wasn't one for keeping her emotions or feelings in check.

At least till she was sure.

'Daniil's here!'

Rachel's voice came down the narrow hall and as Libby brushed her teeth and topped up her lipstick she forced out a smile. There was so much pinned on tonight and she truly wanted to focus on the two of them, aside from everything else.

She walked down the hall. Rachel had let him in and he stood in her hallway and back in her life. The trouble with seeing so little of him was that each time she did, Libby was reminded in detail of his beauty.

The last time he had been in jeans and unshaven, his hair a touch too long. Tonight said hair was smoothed back but longer than she remembered. He still had the designer stubble and his skin was as pale as hers but without that English trace of peaches and cream. Even his scar seemed devoid of colour now.

'When did you get back?' she asked.

'A couple of hours ago.'

His beauty, his demeanour, his guarded approach—she had not even known what country he was in till now—all daunted her.

No kiss, Daniil noted as she went for her bag.

No leaping into his arms, no guided tour of the house.

Just a scowl hurled at him by Rachel as a rather tense Libby wished her goodnight.

'Your flatmate doesn't approve of me,' Daniil said as they drove to the restaurant.

'She's just…' Libby shrugged. Maybe now was the time to tell him how hard tonight would be for her but then she glanced over and decided against it, quite sure that he wouldn't understand.

It was strained, it was awkward and yet it had absolutely nothing to do with him. As she took her seat in the restaurant Libby didn't know if it was the thought of watching *Firebird* or the scent of garlic coming from the kitchen that had her stomach hovering close to her throat.

'Are you looking forward to the ballet?' he asked.

'Of course.' She pushed out a smile as she read through the menu. 'The costumes are supposed to be fantastic.'

The waiter hovered and Daniil wanted to tell him to give them ten minutes but if they were going to make it in time for the show then they needed to order now. He skimmed the menu as Libby deliberated.

'I'd like the scallops…' she started, and then stopped when she saw that the dish she'd chosen would be served on a butter bean sauce—from the tightening of her throat clearly her stomach didn't approve. She wanted something plain and so changed her mind and chose the risotto but then read it had goat's cheese and that made her want to gag too. 'Actually—' Libby called the waiter back '—I'll have consommé.'

'And for the main?' the waiter asked, but Libby shook her head. 'Just the consommé for me.'

'Clear soup for dinner?' Daniil frowned, remembering her comment about her appetite fading whenever she was anxious or stressed.

'Please, don't lecture me about eating.' Libby's response was tart.

He was trying not to, but she looked very pale and he saw the flash of tears in her eyes and he was quite sure it was down to him. Daniil had seen the cautious look on Rachel's face when she had opened the door to him and George's words were still like a worm in his ear. It would seem that Libby Tennent was no longer happy.

No, it wasn't a brilliant dinner.

And despite the most sumptuous company, and chocolates to boot, as well as the very best seats at the ballet, as Libby stared at the curtain that would soon part all she felt was that she was on the wrong side of it.

It had been a mistake to come tonight, she knew as she looked through the programme. The biographies made her want to weep, the sound of the orchestra taking their seats, the air of anticipation all made her want to run for home.

She turned to him, to tell him that this was possibly the worst place on earth that she could be right now.

'Can we just…?' Libby's words were halted by an announcement, telling the audience that the part of the Firebird would tonight be performed by the understudy Tatania Ilyushin.

It was like rubbing salt into the wound for Libby. She looked through the programme and saw that the dancer usually played one of the thirteen princesses. Tonight Tatania had her chance to shine—it was the breakthrough Libby had long dreamed of as her career had started to fade.

Daniil, on best first-date behaviour, though wondering how long it would go on for, stifled a yawn and glanced down at his own programme. The second he turned the page his head tightened as he looked into pale green eyes and remembered a little girl being sent by her mother to get the box that held the tape.

It couldn't be Anya, surely?

Yes, it could.

Tatania might be her full name, or a stage name perhaps. He had never known Anya's surname. Sergio's wife had told him that Anya had done well and had moved to St Petersburg and that Katya had moved there to be closer to her daughter.

He glanced at Libby but her attention was now on the stage, watching as the curtain drew back.

It was stunning, Libby thought as she saw the smoke swirling around the trees on the stage.

And far, far too late to leave without making a small scene.

She peered into the dark forest, waiting for the lights to lift further, but they didn't and she strained to see, wondering if there was a problem. But then a streak of burnt orange flew across the stage, and the audience gasped as Tatania's entrance was made. Graceful, reed thin, Libby knew that if she never ate another piece of cheese in her life and exercised and trained for every minute of every hour she could still never achieve the amazing lines that this dancer made.

She was surely too tall, Libby thought as she attempted a critical eye, yet her arms were like wings without feathers, and it was as if Tatania was truly flying. She spun in the prince's arms—fragile, tiny and seductive—and Libby sat grieving for her own dreams. She had been wrong to come. It was far too soon, a torture of her own making. Yes, it might sound selfish and self-absorbed but that was what it took to make it as far as Tatania had. For Libby it had killed her to leave it behind.

It was a relief when the interval came.

For ten seconds.

'She's amazing,' Daniil said, as did the people standing behind them. As did the people to the left.

'Do you know…?' he started, but how could he tell Libby here? How could he say that possibly the leading lady might know something about his twin?

If it even was Anya.

And if it was, would she even remember him?

Libby could sense his distraction and chewed on the slice of lemon that had come with her water—she didn't dare risk gin, not just because she might well be pregnant, more for the hopeless tears it might produce. Still, the lemon matched the sourness in her mouth and she was about to bite the bullet and suggest that they leave when Daniil drained his drink and spoke.

'I'll be back in a moment.'

He might never have been to the ballet but he was very used to getting his demands met and after a few enquiries he was told that, certainly, they would relay a message to Tatania, asking her to meet him afterwards.

As Daniil went to give his name, he hesitated, wondering if Anya would remember him, given that he had left the orphanage when he was twelve. She had only really come in on her school holidays, he thought.

She would remember the Zverev twins, though, surely?

It was his best chance of being allowed backstage.

'Tell her that one half of the Zverev twins is here and would like to congratulate her personally.'

'Would you like us to organise flowers?'

Daniil accepted. He had not a clue as to protocol in the dancing world and nodded grateful thanks for the suggestion.

Libby stood, biting down tears as the bell went and it was time to take their seats again. Tonight was supposed to be about them, about working things through. Yes, she was well aware that she hadn't been the best company, but did she deserve him walking off and leaving her alone? She looked at the happy couples, all hand in hand, heading back for the second half. Yes, Libby thought as she saw Daniil approaching, gesturing for her to hurry up, she had been a fool to come.

'Where the hell were you?' she asked, but there was no time for a reply as they were being ushered to take their seats quickly.

'I'll tell you later,' Daniil said, just as the curtain went up.

'Do you get a thrill out of keeping me waiting?' she whispered.

'I said that I—' he started, but was shushed by a woman behind them.

Yes, he had left her standing, and as soon as he had a proper chance he would explain.

All of it.

Tatania truly came into her own in the second half.

Maybe next month, or next year, Libby would be delighted that she'd witnessed such an amazing performance, that she'd been there the night Tatania Ilyushin had been discovered by the world.

She was holding back tears as she clapped and Tatania curtsied, scooping up flowers, and Libby didn't like the jealous part of her but, yes, here it was, sitting on her shoulder and whispering dark thoughts.

She couldn't get out quickly enough.

She took her bag, but as she turned to go Daniil was speaking with one of the ushers.

'Come on,' he said.

'Where…?'

He didn't answer and they were led down stairs and through a rabbit warren of corridors, pausing so that he could pull a hefty tip out of his wallet and collect a huge bouquet of flowers.

She wanted to stop him. Really! Was this supposed to be some sort of special treat?

Meet the cast!

Come on, Libby, come and see, up close, exactly what you didn't achieve.

'Daniil…' She stopped dead outside a dressing room, like an angry donkey refusing to budge. When she saw Tatania's name she wanted to turn and run but it was simply too late.

He pushed the door open and there, about to remove her make-up, was, she presumed, another ex-lover of Daniil's.

Libby knew that for certain as Tatania looked into the mirror and saw him and let out a small keening cry as if she had mourned Daniil forever.

That sound had come from her soul and Libby watched as Tatania jumped up and turned around and ran to his arms.

Oh, they'd been lovers, Libby knew, because the dancer's arms wrapped around him and her mouth did not seek, it just homed in, but possibly the words said in Russian by Daniil warned her of the company they were in and Tatania's shoulders drooped briefly and she rapidly stepped back.

'Libby,' Daniil said, 'this is Tatania…'

As if Libby didn't know.

'Excuse me,' Tatania said in a husky voice, 'but I have not seen Daniil in a very long time.'

What was she supposed to say here? Libby wondered.

Not that they would notice—they were back to speaking in Russian, voicing low urgent words until Libby could stand it no more.

He was cruel.

Unnecessarily cruel.

No, Russian wolves weren't kind, she decided there and then. Russian wolves were beautiful and beguiling and the most dangerous of them all.

She had started to believe in him.

And though she'd been warned both about him and by him, she had chosen to believe in good. She knew that she hadn't been at her sparkling best tonight, but she also knew that she didn't deserve this. Was this Daniil's idea of a good night out, to bring her backstage, to point out what she could never be and throw in one of his ex-lovers to boot?

She walked out of the dressing room, salty rivers of tears falling down her cheeks as she turned and looked at the empty corridor behind her. She didn't need to run. Daniil was so locked in conversation with Tatania that he hadn't even noticed that she had gone.

CHAPTER THIRTEEN

IT WASN'T JUST because she was unable to face Rachel and her 'I told you so' that she asked the taxi to take her to the studio.

It was more that she had to know.

Letting herself in, Libby locked the door behind her and, without turning on the main light, raced through to the back, opened her locker and took out the pregnancy test kit.

In the tiny loo she flicked on the light and read the instructions. In three minutes she'd find out, if her shaking hand could just hold the stick steady. She kicked off her panties and did the deed and then stepped out.

She couldn't watch.

Instead, she headed to the dark studio and paced but, really, it wasn't the result that had her heart in her mouth and her nerves in shreds, it was being in love with a consummate bastard. It was the next forty or fifty years, or however long she had left on this planet, to get through without him.

Oh, but she would, she vowed.

And she'd listen to Rachel and have acting lessons if she had to just so she could address him airily if the need arose.

'Yes, it's your baby but not your problem…' She would practise those words till she could look him in the eye and say them, she would…

And then she had the most horrible vision of arriving in Reception with his screaming baby and being pointed in the direction of a creche…a creche filled to the brim with dark-haired, dark-eyed babies and all the other harried mothers who'd succumbed to that devilish charm.

And yet, despite visions and fears, there was want there, too, for that little pink cross and a baby that was his, for a piece of him she could keep, because he had her heart. From the moment she'd walked into his office she might as well have tied up her heart in a pink satin bow and placed it on his desk.

A baby was the only gift he'd ever give, Libby thought.

She'd had to practically beg for flowers.

And then she heard him.

Or rather she heard the purr of his car and the pull of the handbrake, and just as Daniil had been disconcerted to recognise her legs on a business card, that she knew the sound of his car and the way he slammed the door just about brought her to her knees.

Her heart recognised his footsteps and so did her body because it wanted to run to the door and fling it open and leap to him.

Instead, she sat on the floor, curled into the wall, and hugged her knees not just so that he would not see her—more so that she would not succumb, so she would not give in and hit the snooze button on warning thoughts just for ten more minutes with him.

He was the diet that started tomorrow.

The hope that refused to die.

'Libby.'

His voice was low and rich and annoyingly calm.

Bored even?

'I know you're in there.'

He opened the letterbox and started to speak and she put her fingers in her ears so as not to hear that chocolaty voice that lowered her guard and could make her believe she was mad not to give them a try.

'I know that you're there,' he said through the opening. 'I can see you in the mirror.'

'We're closed!' Libby shouted. 'Go away.'

'If you don't want to talk, fine, you can listen. I'm sorry for what happened back there. It was never my intention to ignore you—'

'It just comes naturally to you, does it? Did it give you a kick?' she shouted, forgetting that *she* was supposed to be ignoring *him* now. 'Were you hoping for a threesome?'

'For God's sake—' Daniil didn't sound so calm now '—open this door.'

'No,' she shouted. 'I just want you gone. Tonight was a huge mistake—I didn't even want to go to the ballet. I knew how much seeing *Firebird* was going to hurt but that you'd do that to me, that you'd take me backstage and introduce me to one of your ex-lovers. Have you any idea how much it hurt, how badly I wanted…?' She could barely get the words out. 'Everything that happened to her tonight I dreamed of for myself and you can call me childish and selfish, I don't care. Tonight hurt, but what you just put me through doesn't even compare…'

Daniil closed his eyes. It had never entered his head that she might not be ready to go to the ballet.

Not for a moment.

Now, though, he could see how hard tonight would have been.

'We're not lovers,' he said. 'We never have been.'

'Liar!'

'I mean it,' he said. 'I knew Anya from the orphanage where I was raised. You know I left there when I was twelve.'

She was so about to be glib, about to ask if that was how they'd all kept warm or passed the time, but decided against it.

'Open the door, Libby.'

'No,' she said, though she did move over to the letterbox. 'I know what I saw, Daniil. She ran to you like…'

Just like I would, she thought.

She ran to you with hope in her heart, just as I would if you dropped into my life ten years from now. And Libby loathed herself for being so weak.

So weak because she was at the closed door and trying hard not to open it.

Instead, she peered through the letterbox and saw that delicious mouth.

'Go,' she said. 'You hurt too much.'

'No.'

'Yes.'

'You're the one who always wants to talk,' Daniil pointed out.

'Well, I don't now.'

'You should have said you weren't ready to go the ballet. That was all you had to do.'

Yes, Libby knew that, but it wasn't just the ballet that had had her emotions in turmoil all week.

'If you had just told me…'

'That's fine, coming from you,' she snapped. 'King of boundaries.'

All that was visible of him was that lovely sulky mouth

and she watched as it stretched into a smile. 'I'm here to talk, Libby.'

'You might not want to hear what I have to say, though.'

Oh, they had a whole lot of talking to do but there was something she had to get off her chest first.

'You remember that you said my technique was all wrong, that I should just lay it all out on the table up-front?'

'I do.' Daniil frowned. He had no idea where this was leading. He had raced through the night to tell her his truth and was instead being asked to listen to what she had to say.

'I haven't been feeling well,' Libby said.

'Okay?'

'My period…'

'Is that why you're teary and irrational?'

'No,' she whispered. She'd deal with his presumption another time. 'It's late.'

She watched as his tongue ran over his lips and then closed her eyes, too scared to look.

'How late?'

His voice sounded very normal, much the way it had when he'd asked her if she'd be using her own savings for the ballet studio, only the stakes were far higher now.

'A week,' Libby said, and when she got no response elaborated, 'That's a lot for me.'

'And how do you feel?'

'Sick,' Libby said.

'Sick with nerves, or sick?'

'Both,' Libby admitted. 'I'm scared.'

'Never, ever be scared when you're near me.'

'You're not cross?'

'Why would I be cross? We were both there when

it happened, we both took the chance. I've told you—I never take risks unless I'm prepared to weather the consequences.'

'You thought about it.'

'Not really,' Daniil said, and now she had the courage to look at his beautiful mouth and see his slight smile. 'But I've never taken such a risk with another woman. Libby, whether you are pregnant or not, you don't need to be scared.'

'But I do. I've just started my own business…' Tears were taking over again and Daniil listened to them. He could step in, tell her she had nothing to worry about, that even if she didn't want him, the money would be taken care of, yet he knew that right now it was about her.

That Libby needed to know that she would be okay.

Herself.

'I'd have to employ someone or close and I was just getting started, it's too soon…'

'Libby!' He broke into her mounting panic. 'Do you know why my business plans work so well, why the banks always say yes to me?'

'No.'

'Because I'm a pessimist. The bank knows that I don't put a positive spin on things. I factor in things like illness and pregnancy and women who leap to the worst possible conclusion and shut up shop because their soon-to-be ex might have slept with a ballerina a decade or so ago…'

She started to smile because she had been thinking exactly that—wondering how she could work while her heart was breaking, how she could dance and smile if she found she had a baby on board and no longer had him.

'You really think I can do it?'

'Of course. I wouldn't have put my name to it otherwise.'

She was calm, not as calm as she had been in that sugary haze in his hotel suite, but the panic was fading.

'You're very good in a crisis.'

'I am,' Daniil said. 'It's the normal stuff that I don't do so well with—like flowers and calling and letting you know the day-to-day stuff in my life. Will you let me in?'

She stood there.

'You're asking the same of me, Libby,' Daniil pointed out. 'You're asking me to let you in, and I can't do that from the other side of a door.'

She turned the lock and stepped back, and though she wanted to go into his embrace she remembered how Tatania had and she folded her arms in defence, confused and raw and hurting yet wanting him all the same. 'I don't believe for a moment that you and she weren't lovers.'

'We never were.'

'Daniil, can we move past the lies? I saw the way she ran to you.'

'Did you notice the way her shoulders sagged?' he demanded. 'Did you see her recoil, or her expression when I stepped out of the shadows and she saw my scar?'

'I don't understand.'

'She thought that I was Roman.'

'Roman?' Libby blinked. 'Why would she…?' Even as she asked, she knew the answer.

'Roman is my twin.'

She felt as if all the air had been sucked out of the room as he spoke on.

'My identical twin,' Daniil said. 'For a moment, Anya, I mean Tatania, thought that I was him. I think you're right. I think something must have gone on between them after I left the orphanage.'

'They separated you?' Libby could hear the horror in her voice as she struggled to comprehend what had happened. 'They didn't let you keep in touch?'

'My parents never sent him the letters I wrote.'

Libby stood there, her head spinning, and Daniil mistook her silence.

'I messed up tonight,' he said. 'When I saw—'

'No, no,' she said, for she understood now. 'I'm surprised you didn't storm the stage and demand answers.'

'I had other things on my mind, too,' Daniil said.

'Like?'

'A very unhappy date. I thought I was making you miserable.'

'No.'

'You could have told me it was too soon for the ballet.'

'I'm glad I've been now,' she said. 'And Tatania was amazing. Why would you think you made me miserable? You know I'm crazy about you, I've never attempted to hide it.'

'I listened to my cousin. He reminded me how miserable I made the family.'

'Rubbish!' Libby said. 'They were miserable and messed up long before you arrived.'

'You don't know that.'

'Oh, but I do,' she said. 'Marcus has been with them for thirty years...' And she told him that Marcus had been ready to leave until a twelve-year-old orphan had arrived in a very unhappy home. 'He felt he couldn't leave you to deal with them.' Her eyes filled with tears. 'I can't believe they didn't send your letters, that they took you from him.'

'It's okay,' Daniil said to her obvious upset. He'd had many years to get used to the facts that Libby was only now trying to understand.

'No, it's not okay!' she said, furious and hurting on his behalf, and then she told him not what perhaps she should say, just exactly what she felt. 'We'll find him.'

They were the best three words he had ever heard for they were delivered with the same urgency and passion that he felt. Whether finding Roman was possible or not, it was the priority she afforded it that sealed his love. For the first time since the orphanage there was *we* rather than *I*, and it meant she would reside in his heart forever.

'We'll find him,' Libby said again, and she didn't try to fight her feelings anymore—she simply flew to arms that lifted her, accepted her. And she had been right that first morning. She *could* live on his hips because her legs coiled around him and his face was near hers and it was better than being home. 'We're going to find him,' she said, with the hope he'd been starting to lose.

'I've tried.'

'We'll keep trying.' And it hit Libby then, the *we* word, because she knew they were the future, as easily as breathing; somehow her mind accepted they were in each other's lives forever. 'Who's the eldest?'

'We don't know,' Daniil said.

And with that answer Libby glimpsed a world without a foundation.

'We were going to be boxers—that was going to be our ticket out of poverty—but then the Thomases made enquiries about me. I didn't want to be adopted but Roman insisted that I go. We had a fight… He said he would do better in the ring without me. I know now he was just trying to ensure I took my chance…'

'That's how you got the scar?' she asked, and Daniil gave no shake of his head to warn that that question was out of bounds. Instead, he nodded.

She put her fingers up to the jagged flesh and understood now why he had kept it as it was—it was the mark of his brother's love for him and he wore it with pride.

'We'll find your family,' she said.

'I have a family now,' Daniil said. 'You.'

Then Libby forgot; she forgot they had problems, she forgot all that was wrong with the world because all was right in hers as he held her in his arms and they kissed. It was a different kiss from any of their others. This kiss was theirs, nothing held back and no leader—they were in this race together. She kissed him back and he kissed her forward, deep, hungry kisses that had waited too long.

'You turn me on...' Libby breathed into his mouth, wrapping herself around him even tighter.

'I thought I couldn't ignore you all night and expect...' He stopped because as his hand slipped up her dress he felt naked buttocks. 'No underwear...' He was at her neck, marking it; she could feel it and she wanted his mark.

'I was...'

Oh, she'd forgotten everything—even the most important thing had flitted away.

'I was doing a test...'

Between hungry kisses she pointed and he carried her through to the tiny area and the light went on but Libby didn't see it. Her face was buried in his neck as her hands worked his zipper and the only thing that really mattered was the two of them.

'You are.'

He told her she was pregnant and then kissed her

hard enough to chase away any thoughts of too soon, too much. It was good news and they sure as hell deserved it.

Oh, didn't becoming a parent make you suddenly responsible? Instead, she was back in a dance studio with her shoulders against a mirror and her hands holding the barre in a way she never had before.

There was nothing other than the sound of desperate sex and Libby could no longer hold on. He pulled her flush to his torso and she wrapped her arms round his head and sobbed as he started to come.

Yes, naughty toes, because hers curled as every muscle squeezed to his tune yet he was no puppeteer—there were no strings, and she danced free in his arms.

'You're pregnant.' He said it while still inside her. When they should have been coming down from a high, they just stepped from one cloud to the next. 'Are you happy?'

'So happy,' she said. 'You?'

'More,' Daniil said, because his family had just got bigger.

They shared the sweetest kiss and then he tried to put her down but she refused. 'I don't want to let you go.'

She was over-the-top, way too affectionate, yet everything he hadn't known he needed.

'I'm going to love you so much,' Libby said.

'Then, I'd better take you home.'

CHAPTER FOURTEEN

'When did you first know you loved me?' Libby asked as they stepped into his home.

'I haven't told you I love you.'

'Oh, please…' she dismissed. 'So come on, when?'

She was nothing like he was used to but then again he wasn't used to smiling, either, but he was doing that now as she prowled around his home.

Yes, he smiled at the slight sag in her shoulders as she looked at his bookshelf and he knew she was annoyed that the *thing* she had brought him wasn't there.

And neither was it in the bedroom when she peered in.

'Did the cleaner move it?'

'Move what?' he teased.

'I can't believe you got rid of my first present to you.' She pouted. 'I've the napkin from our first dinner.'

'Seriously?'

'Yes…and I've pressed three of the flowers you gave me and…'

She went into her handbag and produced a little bar of very exclusive soap.

'That's from my bathroom.'

'I know. I went through your cupboards and took one. I

wanted a memento of our *one* night.' She almost stamped her foot. 'You really are the most unsentimental man.'

'There's something for you in the kitchen.'

That put a smile on her face and for the first time in living memory Libby ran into a room she usually tried to run from and there on the bench was a box.

'You got me a present.'

'I did,' Daniil said. 'I got it in Russia and I had it wrapped, but it was opened at customs. I was going to have Cindy rewrap it on Monday. As you can see, I tried…'

There was more sticky tape than one box could handle, and Libby rightly guessed that choosing presents and wrapping gifts wasn't something he'd done much of in his life.

'Can I open it?'

'Do.'

Daniil was as tense as she'd been when he had opened her gift, and he glimpsed then how things like this mattered, how choosing something for someone you loved meant you so badly wanted them to love it, too.

'There aren't any gift shops where I come from and I didn't want to just get something from the airport.' He could hear the rare tension in his own voice as she opened it. 'Sergio's wife knew someone who was an accomplished glassblower. I watched this being made.'

Her hand was shaking as she opened the box and there was her *thing* from him—a slender ballet dancer in glass, with blue eyes and a wide smile.

'And she has a hole in her head for a flower!' Libby cried out in delight. 'I love it, I love her, it's the best gift I've ever had and you must have loved me then…'

'Maybe,' he relented. 'Or maybe a bit before that.' He guided her to the room she hadn't been allowed to enter before, and just as he had opened her bedroom door, Libby opened this one and entered his private space.

'You did keep it.' She smiled, because once her eyes had taken in all the gym equipment, she looked over to a shelf and there that glittery porcelain ornament sat.

She placed her glass ballerina next to it and then saw she belonged beside the only other possessions that mattered to him.

She reached up and took the picture down and Daniil stood behind her, looking at the photo of four young boys.

'You look like brothers,' Libby commented, because they all had dark hair and pale skin and solemn eyes.

'I know, but only Roman and I are related. I didn't even know I had these with me when I came. Roman must have slipped them into my case. I had copies made and sent them to him but, of course, they were never posted.'

How cruel, Libby thought.

'My parents tried to throw these out,' he said, 'but Marcus retrieved them and kept them for me.'

And then she said it.

'They're not your parents,' Libby said. 'They don't deserve that title.'

'You don't hold back, do you?'

'I'll try...'

'Never hold back,' he said, and then he looked down at the photo. 'That's Sev.' He pointed to a serious-looking child.

'The one who the letter was from?' Libby asked, and she turned her head and he nodded.

'You'll find him.'

'Maybe.'

'So that must be Nikolai.'

There was a long stretch of silence and then he ran a

finger over the image of a young life lost and his voice was a husk.

'Yes.'

'How did he drown?'

'He was found in a river,' Daniil said. 'He ran away because he was being abused.' He closed his eyes and she was patient with his silence and then he opened them again. 'And there's Roman,' he said, but he did not point. Daniil waited for her to try to guess which one of the twins he was. 'You won't be able to tell us apart, no one was ever able to.'

'I can.'

She pointed to the boy on the left. 'That's you.'

'Fluke,' Daniil said. 'Look at this one.'

He took down the other photo and she looked at two serious boys with black hair and dark eyes, and it had been taken before the scar on his cheek…

Again she chose correctly.

'How do you know?'

'I just know,' Libby said. 'I guess that's love.'

She watched as he put the photos down beside the letter. The *thing* she had given him seemed to smile and say it would keep them safe.

'Come on,' he said.

This time when they moved to the bedroom it was hand in hand, and as she walked into the vast space another question she had was answered.

She stilled as she heard through the night the chimes as Big Ben struck midnight. It made her shiver low in her stomach. The room that had looked so empty seemed to fill with the low and beautifully familiar noise and Libby wondered how she had missed it their first night.

Daniil watched her mouth open as it did and he saw

that tiny frown and he knew her question without her voicing it.

'On a still night you can hear them,' he said. 'I had the glass modified so that sometimes you can hear them chime. It is very nice to fall asleep or wake up to.'

'You *are* sentimental,' she said.

'I am,' Daniil said. 'And the answer to your question is nine o'clock.'

'Sorry?' Libby frowned.

'Fifteen hours after you walked into my office, and fifteen minutes after you walked out of my home, the clock struck nine and I guess I was already in love with you because I called Cindy and told her to cancel my morning so I could work on your business plan. So,' Daniil asked, curious now, 'when did you know you loved me?'

'What's the time, Mr Wolf?'

Daniil frowned at her game.

'Six o'clock.' Libby answered with the truth.

The moment I saw you I knew.

EPILOGUE

'I HATE YOU,' Rachel said, as she added the last curl to Libby's hair.

'I know you do.' Libby smiled.

In half an hour's time she would be marrying the man of her dreams and Rachel was going to be a witness.

Wrapped in her dressing gown, Libby took one last look around the flat. It was a lot emptier now as over the past few weeks her things had been moved over to Daniil's, but now she gave her flatmate and friend a hug before she finally moved out.

'You've been the best friend…'

'Don't get all sentimental,' Rachel warned. 'I've just done your make-up.'

'I know.' Libby smiled but then it wavered. 'I'm so nervous…'

'Why?' Rachel asked. 'You're head over heels and not afraid to show it.'

'I know. I'm just worried what everyone's going to say when they find out we're married and…' Libby screwed her eyes closed. 'I don't care what they say.'

Oh, she did.

A bit.

Her father would freak at the missed opportunity to

organise such a potentially prominent wedding. After all, the press were going to go crazy when they found out that Daniil Zverev was married and that his bride was pregnant.

'It wouldn't be fair to Daniil to have a big family wedding when his own brother can't be there.' Rachel reminded Libby of the reason they had chosen the quietest of celebrations. 'Do you feel as if you're missing out?'

'Missing out?' Libby's mouth gaped. 'This is my idea of a perfect wedding.'

It was.

Libby looked in the mirror once she had put on her dress—it was very simple, a soft ivory and more like a silk slip than a designer gown, but to her it was perfect.

She put on new soft ballet shoes and she had a bunch of palest pink peonies, roses and calla lilies, and she'd added anemones, too, because she'd loved them first.

'Am I showing?' Libby asked, because she was desperate to get a bump but it was still way too soon.

'You're only ten weeks,' Rachel pointed out.

They had been the happiest weeks of both hers and Daniil's lives.

'Do you think he's guessed about your surprise?' Rachel asked.

'No.' Libby smiled as they got into the car and Rachel drove them to the registry office.

They wouldn't be getting some random witness. Instead, Libby had called Marcus, and he and his own new wife Shirley were coming to the wedding today before they headed off on a cruise.

They were family, Libby had decided as the car pulled up and there, waiting, was Daniil.

'You don't look nervous,' she said, as he took her hand.

'Wolves are never nervous,' Daniil said. 'Anyway, why would I be anything other than happy today?'

Why indeed?

They walked into the old building and he stilled and the calm, always composed Daniil was at a loss for words when he saw Marcus and Shirley waiting for them.

'Thank you,' Daniil said to the man who had stepped in, who had guarded his precious photos for him and had respected his space.

'We wouldn't miss this for the world,' Marcus said.

It really was the tiniest of weddings, but it was loaded with love.

The least sentimental man put a ring on her finger, dotted with pink argyle diamonds, just because it was her favourite colour in the world.

'I love you.' He said words he'd never thought he would. 'And I will make sure you know that every day. You will always be my leading lady.'

It was her favourite role and one she could only have dreamed of till now. There in the spotlight of his love Libby felt she could fly.

'And I love you,' she said. 'I always will.'

There was cake for everyone, made by Shirley again, only this time without resentment so it tasted divine, and there was champagne for everyone except the bride, who didn't need bubbles to be fizzing with joy.

And then it was just them, husband and wife checking into a lavish London hotel with a different view, one that looked out at the palace where tomorrow they would sit at midday and wait and see if Sev came.

'I don't think he'll be there,' Daniil said, because tomorrow was five years to the day he should have met him.

'He might be,' Libby said. 'It's worth a try.'

'It is,' Daniil said.

Love was *always* worth the try, he'd now found out.

Love was the most precious gift and, Daniil found, with love had come hope.

He closed the drapes on the view and the possibilities of tomorrow as he focused on this special night.

He took his bride in his arms and Libby lifted her face to meet his kiss.

Tomorrow they would look for answers.

Tonight, though, for Daniil and Libby there were no questions, just the tender celebration of their love.

* * * * *

If you've read and loved gorgeous Daniil,
don't miss the second book in
IRRESISTIBLE RUSSIAN TYCOONS,
the scandalous new quartet from Carol Marinelli!
THE COST OF THE FORBIDDEN
available January 2016 from Harlequin Presents

Maisey Yates

Christmas at The Chatsfield

Lucy Kennewick hated Christmas. She had for the past five years. Every single year she had spent in her husband's—soon-to-be ex-husband's—sterile mansion, void of boughs of holly, mistletoe or anything resembling a reindeer, had been bleak and soulless like the man himself.

Before her marriage to Nico she had quite liked Christmas in New York. From the beautiful department-store window displays to the glittering tree in Rockefeller Center. But after that all of the festive cheer outside had only been a reminder of the starkness inside her life.

She lifted the red skirt of her gown as she walked up the steps that led to the front entrance to the grand ballroom of the Chatsfield. This would be her first Christmas party without him since they were married, and she was determined to enjoy herself.

They had both been invited. Because when the invitations had been sent out their marriage had still been seamless, as far as the public eye was concerned.

Though, the iconic marriage of Lucy Kennewick and Nico Katsaros had never been all that it had appeared.

A marriage to shore up her failing company. A marriage of convenience.

Though, a *real* marriage. In spite of the fact they had never shared a room, never shared their personal space, they had most certainly shared a bed.

As Lucy walked into the ballroom she unbuttoned her long black coat, handing it to the man waiting to check it. As she did she became suddenly conscious of her hands, of the fact that her left hand was bare. That her ring was gone.

That her marriage was over.

She should be happy. The day after Christmas everything would be finalized, and her life would go back to normal. Her marriage to Nico would be nothing more than a blip on the radar. A starter marriage. Who in the city didn't have one of those?

She made her way deeper into the room, feeling suddenly very conscious in the bright red silk gown amid the sea of chic New York City black. The annual Christmas ball was always a can't-miss event, but since the takeover of the new CEO, interest had been heightened. So many of the people here were in attendance because they were searching for something. For a sign of weakness, for a way to ally with Spencer Chatsfield. And Lucy?

Lucy simply wanted to take this chance to start over.

But she had one thing in common with the rest of the guests. She was wearing a mask over her eyes, offering the thinnest veil of anonymity. Making her feel as though she was watching all of those around her, while keeping herself hidden from them.

Suddenly she felt a prickling sensation on the back of her neck and she lifted her head, looking into a mirror that was mounted on the wall in front of her. She could see herself, dark hair styled into loose waves, the golden mask fitted to her face, red lips, painted to match the crimson gown that formed to her slight curves, parted as if in shock.

And then she saw what had caused the prickling sensation. She had been wrong. She had been seen. Someone else was watching her. In the reflection of the mirror, her eyes connected to those of the man behind her. He was wearing a black mask, his flawless body outlined to perfection in the custom-made suit he was wearing.

Those dark eyes saw through her mask. And she saw through his.

Nico Katsaros. Her first husband. Her first lover, but never her first love. Because he didn't believe in it. And she didn't want it.

The ghost of Christmas past had come to haunt her indeed.

His wife was here. And she had the nerve to look like every Christmas present he'd been denied as a child.

Then, as now, seeing the brightly wrapped gift, all he wanted to do was to tear back the paper and reveal the treasure beneath. Then, as now, he was forbidden from doing so.

The child of a maid living in a palatial estate, he had witnessed grandeur on a massive scale from a very early age. Witnessed it, but not been allowed to partake of it.

He hated being denied. Then and now.

She was beautiful, Lucy was. She always had been. And when she had proposed a marriage of convenience between the two of them to help improve his playboy image, and to add her ailing company to his list of assets, he had been more than willing. A wife was the next logical acquisition for him, and one as beautiful as Lucy could never be a hardship.

Tonight she had outdone herself. The gown was beautiful, but he was fixated on what the pale skin beneath it looked like. He knew. He knew intimately. The silky texture, every delicate curve of her body.

He and Lucy had always been able to talk business, and they had always been able to make love.

It was everything else they found challenging.

Sex had never been an issue. He had wondered at first, because when he'd met Lucy she had seemed quite severe. All business. And yet, the way her suits had been tailored to her exquisite body had given him a hint that she was a woman who knew her appeal and also knew how to use it.

During their very short engagement they had discovered that the business arrangement was not the only perk of their union. Their attraction had been combustible from the beginning. Though, she had made him wait for their wedding night, and he had been rewarded spectacularly with her innocence and the most explosive encounter of his life.

Every encounter thereafter had only been better. And for five years, even as he felt the gulf widen between them their physical intimacy had only grown more intense.

Until she had told him she was leaving. Until she had told him it was over.

After that, all of the lust he had felt had turned into burning, brilliant hatred. As white-hot as any passion that had ever passed between them before.

Though, seeing her now, he knew that not all of the lust between them had been eradicated.

Crystal blue eyes met his in the reflection of the mirror and he began to walk toward her. The same eyes widened in horror, her lush red lips pressing into a firm line. She did not want him to talk to her. All the more reason to approach.

"Merry Christmas, *agape mou*."

Those words. Oh, dear God, those words. They had always ignited a fire in her stomach. And parts lower.

"It isn't Christmas yet, Nico." She swallowed hard, bracing herself to turn and face him, to deal with the man in the flesh rather than as a ghost reflected before her. "There are still a few hours left."

She turned, and realized too late that there was no bracing herself for impact when it came to him. Her only consolation was that the mask blunted some of his masculine beauty, the black leather concealing his strong brow and his cheekbones. But it did nothing to reduce the intensity of his dark gaze. And it certainly didn't stop her stomach from tightening painfully. Didn't stop her body from responding.

Five years she had shared his bed and nothing had taken the edge off of her desire for him.

Not even when she had grown bitter, broken over the distance that remained between them.

No matter how many times she kissed him, no matter how many times she let him inside her body, she never felt closer to him. They had sex, but they did not have intimacy. And there came a point where she could no longer bear it.

"You wouldn't know it. Based on the department-store displays, one would assume Christmas began in October."

"And yet, I would venture to say that based on our

own work schedules you wouldn't know it was Christmas at all."

"What are you doing with your time these days, Lucy?"

Since you no longer have your company. The rest of the sentence remained unspoken.

She had lost Kennewick Manufacturing when she had chosen to divorce Nico. But among the many things she had learned about herself over the past few years was the fact that she now knew business couldn't fill every void. She needed more. And in order to have more, she had to escape her marriage.

"Right now? Volunteer work. I haven't decided anything about my future yet. It may surprise you to know that I'm eminently employable."

He chuckled, the dark sound rolling over her like a hit of good alcohol, warming her, making her light-headed. "That doesn't surprise me at all. You have a keen business mind, even if you are a faithless wife."

"I was never once unfaithful to you, Nico."

"Betraying your marriage vows by seeking divorce is not unfaithful?"

Lucy gritted her teeth. "Divorce is legal. I was your wife, not your prisoner."

"As the holidays have slowed things up you are still my wife."

She looked down, swallowing, or rather, trying to. Her throat was so dry she felt as though she had been snacking on cotton balls. "Yes, well, another reason to dislike this time of year."

"Perhaps you should speak to our host Spencer Chatsfield about getting a job? I'm sure the new CEO of the Chatsfield Empire would be delighted to have you. The rumor is that he is out to acquire the Harrington chain of hotels as well, so I imagine there will be more job opportunities open for those who are already in house. One would think those at the Harrington will be out of luck."

"Why would you think I'd have any interest in that?"

"Because you have a thing for powerful men, and Spencer Chatsfield is most certainly that."

Rage zipped down her spine. "Is that what you think of me? That the only way I could possibly get ahead is to use a man?"

"Your track record would suggest that as a possibility," he said, his voice hard. "However, you are wrong. It is not what I think of you. Because I do not think of you at all."

The lie burned his tongue. He thought of her. He thought of her every night as he tried to sleep. He'd thought of her when he tried to pick up a woman in a club only a few nights ago. He thought of nothing but Lucy. His body wanted no woman but Lucy.

Inconvenient, since he despised Lucy.

Their life had been comfortable, until she had left. Nothing had changed. He had not changed.

She had changed.

She had left him. And he was not done with her.

Standing there right now, looking at her in that dress, his fingers itching to tear it from her body, he *knew* he was not done with her.

The mask did nothing to dull her beauty. If anything, it added mystery.

Mystery. That was intriguing, considering the fact she had been in his bed for five years, considerably longer than any other woman in his life ever had been. And he had been faithful to her. He had not been certain he could manage that when they'd first married. But it had been easy. He'd never wanted anyone else.

Which was the issue now, considering she was no longer his wife, or rather, wouldn't be on the day after Christmas.

But he had let her walk out. He had let her do so without a fight.

He had let her get away too easy. Perhaps being married to her had made him soft. In the past no one would have dared to find Nico Katsaros in that way.

He had allowed Lucy to make him forget who he was.

And it was time that both she, and he, remembered.

"Do you know, as we have been standing here talking I find I'm remembering something," he said.

"What?" she asked.

"I am very angry with you."

"You are angry with me?" Her blue eyes flashed with rage. "You think you have the right to be angry with me?"

"Oh yes, I have every right. You made vows to me, *agape*. And you have broken them."

"Why should you care? It isn't as though you love me."

Her words hung between them, resting just below the soft strains of Christmas music that were drifting through the air.

"I do not have to love you to want you," he said.

"It would be nice if you didn't hate me."

"The sex was very hot between us when our feelings were much more bland. Imagine how good it could be now."

Her pale cheeks flushed red. "That's neither here nor there, as having sex with the man you are divorcing is hardly advisable."

"But you are wearing a mask. As am I. We could be anyone."

"But we are not," she said, her breasts rising on a sharp breath.

"So serious, Lucy," he said. "Always. Much too serious."

"Life is serious. You have never seemed to take it that way."

"Obviously you don't know me very well, Lucy."

Furious blue eyes met his. "Whose fault is that?"

"It doesn't matter. Not if we are strangers."

He let the words simmer there for a moment.

The fire in her eyes chilled, crystallized. "What exactly are you proposing?"

"That we leave the past here. And go upstairs and have one last night together. One last Christmas. You look every inch like a present just for me, and I find I cannot wait to unwrap you."

Lucy could only stare at her husband, stunned.

Nico was holding out forbidden fruit, and she desperately wanted to grab hold of it. To do more than simply take a bite. To seize it, to savor it.

But even as she battled her desire to speak the *yes* that hovered on her lips, her insides curled in on themselves, retreating as though they'd been touched by fire.

Because she remembered why she'd asked for the divorce in the first place. Because she remembered that sex—no matter how good—couldn't replace real, emotional intimacy. That it wouldn't fill the emptiness in her, or fix the loneliness that always hit her with the force of a hurricane after they finished making love and Nico went back to his own bedroom.

Which meant that no matter how intensely her body burned, she could not submit herself to that kind of pain. Not again.

"This *present* is no longer for you."

His dark eyes burned into hers. "Is that so? Is someone else going to open you up this year, *agape*?"

"Perhaps," she lied.

"Then you must point him out to me," Nico said, his tone hard.

"For what purpose?"

"So that I can kill him."

A strange little zip of pleasure wound its way through her body. Nico was passionate about business, he was passionate in the bedroom, but in his verbal exchanges with her he had never been anything but measured, calm. Disinterested almost. He had certainly never expressed jealousy. And that was what this was, jealousy. Her soon-to-be ex-husband was jealous. Of a fictional man who didn't exist anywhere outside of a tiny little implied falsehood.

"You're *not* going to kill my lover," she said, unable to resist pushing him a little bit further.

"You think not? But then you must ask yourself, Lucy, if you ever knew me."

"If I didn't know you, whose fault was it? Mine or yours, Nico?"

"Perhaps it is both of ours."

She sucked in a sharp breath. "Do you think so? I never kept anything from you."

He reached out, taking hold of her chin to study her face, forcing her eyes to meet his. "Did you not?" His gaze was intense, focused. He slid his thumb along her bottom lip, sending sparks of pleasure along her spine. "I very much believe that you kept secrets from me."

Every guilty word she had left unspoken between them built up inside her chest. "I can't fathom you would have ever cared to hear my secrets."

"So instead you will tell them to another man?"

"What will I get in return if I tell them to you?"

"Pleasure. Have I ever denied you pleasure?"

"No." She blinked hard. "But in the end it wasn't enough."

"For a marriage, perhaps. But for a night?"

She cleared her throat. "Even if I did intend to sleep with another man, you would try to seduce me away from him?"

"If in fact you do intend to sleep with another man tonight, then I am certainly angry with you. But not angry enough to cut off my nose to spite my face, so to speak. And anyway, I would rather have you in my bed than know you were in bed with someone else."

"And what about you? Going back to the legions of women you used to have before you married me?"

"There has been no one else. I want no one else," he said, his voice rough.

"Really?" His words soothed the wound she hadn't been aware was there.

"But it was not the same for you?"

"Of course there is no one else. There was no one before you. Why would I find another lover so quickly after you?"

A slow, satisfied smile spread over his features. And she knew she had made a mistake. Knew that she had forgotten she was talking to a predator. One who saw her as prey.

"Perhaps I should not be so gratified to hear this, but I am."

"That does not mean I'm going to sleep with you."

"All right," he said, his tone measured, calm. She wasn't fooled. "But if you will not sleep with me, perhaps you would consider dancing with me?"

Nico's heart was pounding in his head, the metallic tang of anger only just now receding from his tongue. It had been a lie, and he was grateful for it. She was still his wife, after all, even if it was for only one more day.

After that, once she was no longer his, she could have whomever she wanted. But until then, she belonged to him. If she was spending the night in anyone's bed in these last remaining hours of their marriage, it would be his.

"Dance with me," he repeated.

"Just a dance?"

"If you wish."

He extended his hand, his chest tightening as he evaluated the expression on her face, partially concealed by the golden mask. There was fear in her eyes, trepidation. He had not seen her look at him that way since their wedding night. When she had been a virgin. When she had been filled with uncertainty as to what would pass between them. He had taught her, and quickly, that there was nothing to fear from him, not the marriage bed. And while they had never trusted each other with everything, they had trusted each other physically. He could see that he had lost that during their six months of separation.

But then, she intended to separate from him forever, so perhaps that should not come as a surprise.

"One dance," he said, unable to remain patient. Unable to wait for her to make the next move.

"One." She curled her delicate fingers around his and he fought the urge to cling to her tightly, to tug her against his chest and kiss her now, to prove to her that whatever she believed, whatever she pretended, whatever those signed divorce papers waiting to be filed said, her body still belonged to him.

He resisted, but only just, playing the part of gentleman as he led her out to the dance floor. Everything in him longed to pull her tight against him, and yet he managed to draw her into a respectful closed hold.

Oh yes, he was very much playing the part of the gentleman he'd never been.

The better to lure you into bed, my dear.

She looked up at him, blue eyes wide, as though she had heard the thought. He said nothing, only raising an eyebrow in response.

He was unbearably conscious of the feel of her skin beneath his. And of the fact her hand seemed different somehow.

Her ring. Her ring was gone.

"You have taken off my ring?" he asked.

"Yes. We're divorcing." She looked down and he knew then she'd caught sight of the gold band he still wore on his left hand. "You still wear yours?"

"I was not the one who asked for a divorce," he said, his tone closing the subject neatly.

He didn't want to discuss why he still wore the sign of their commitment, not when he couldn't even explain it to himself.

She looked away and he could see a pulse beating at the base of her throat. He wanted to press his lips to the delicate skin there, feel for himself the effect he was having on her.

It was so rare for him to touch her outside the bedroom. After they'd established themselves as a couple, they had never bothered with such shows of romance. Why would they? Their marriage had never been about that.

Now though…now that he was staring into forever without her, now that he was looking at her, watching her body sway to the music, seeing her dress swirl around her feet, around his legs, a bright shock of crimson against the black suit pants, he regretted it.

He released his hold on her hand, tracing a line down her cheek, meeting her eyes. "How long has it been since we danced?"

Lucy looked away from Nico, trying to get a hold on her senses. They were currently galloping ahead of her like wild horses, her heartbeat keeping time with imaginary hoofbeats. How had she allowed herself to forget the effect he had on her?

She should have known that the moment he touched her she would be lost.

It had been that way from the beginning.

She remembered clearly just before they had announced their engagement how he had demanded they test their chemistry. He was not, he had said, marrying a woman whose bed he had no desire to be in. She had been angry then. Because in her mind passion had nothing to do with their arrangement. For all she cared, he could take mistresses.

At least, that had been her feeling just before his lips had touched hers.

From that moment she had known she would be his, and his alone. And that she would demand he be hers. That kiss had changed something in her, had opened up a well of deep longing she hadn't realized was there. He had made her aware in that moment of how much of life she had been missing pouring herself into her work at the exclusion of all else. Doing her very best to continue on the legacy her father hadn't been able to see through.

After his death when Lucy was nineteen, she had become obsessed with the idea of keeping things going. Of taking the company to the place her father had imagined it could go. But somewhere in all of that, in the midst of trying to live out someone else's dreams, she had lost pieces of herself. Had become hollow, incomplete. And Nico… Teaching her to want again… He had made her so painfully aware of it.

From there, it had been a slow descent into madness. Of becoming increasingly aware of that emptiness until she'd had to change something. Ironically, without Nico she never would have realized the emptiness was there. Ironic, because it was her feelings for him that made her so aware, that made it impossible to stay.

That made it so painful to leave.

Yes, she had told him in the beginning she had no need of love.

She had been a fool.

Because the moment his lips had touched hers five long years ago, she had realized that everything she believed about herself was a lie.

And on her wedding night she had discovered that not only did she desperately want love, craved it, but she wanted it from her husband.

The man who had vowed to stay with her in sickness and in health, for richer or poorer.

The man who had also vowed, after the wedding ceremony, once they were alone, that he would never, ever love her.

Memories of the past echoed through Nico as he twirled his wife around the dance floor. Strange that an action so foreign to them should conjure up memories. More than memories, there was a strange, hollow ache. Of memories that should have been.

He had not taken her dancing. They had danced at their wedding, as they had been expected to do. Once at a gala when they had been establishing their couple status with the public. But never since.

Regret lanced him, stealing his breath. This would be the last time they danced. He had not appreciated that before. Had not fully appreciated all of the things he would never do again with her once they had divorced.

Certainly, there would be other women. Of course there would be. He had not been a monk prior to his marriage, so it stood to reason he would not be after. And yet, the prospect did not fill him with excitement. Not in the least. He did not feel as if he had been unchained from a shackle. Rather, he felt as though he were walking back into a dungeon he had already been freed from once.

A strange feeling. Ridiculous.

And yet, he could not shake it off. Not now he had had it.

He tried to remember the last time they had made love. He had not been conscious of the fact it would be the last time. Her request for a divorce had come out of the blue, during the middle of the day. There had been no opportunity to say goodbye. No opportunity to cement the end of their relationship with a final coupling.

He could no longer let that stand. He could not endure it.

This was to be their last dance. And tonight, Christmas Eve, would be their last night together.

Nico Katsaros was a man who went after what he wanted. And right now he wanted to seduce his wife.

"Good thing we have the masks. We might have caused some gossip otherwise," Lucy said, her voice soft.

"Would that be the worst thing?"

"There would be no truth to the rumors."

"Is there no truth in this?" he asked, taking the opportunity to trace the lush outline of her ruby lips again, her warmth and softness beneath his fingertip a tease he could scarcely withstand.

"Attraction. But we've been down that road. It ends. I ended it."

"It does not end for two more nights. Tonight. We can have tonight."

"Nico…"

And suddenly, he was not content to simply touch her lips. He had to taste them as well.

With the music in the background promising with sincerity that the singer would be home for Christmas, Nico bent his head and kissed his wife.

And for the first time in six months, he did indeed feel as though he was home.

Surely, over the course of five years of marriage, Nico had kissed her thousands of times. But in this moment she forgot them all. She forgot everything but this. But his lips on hers, in this moment. Forgot everything except what a revelation this was.

She clung to him, curling her fingers around the collar of his suit jacket, holding him to her, afraid that this moment, this man, would disappear back into the ether if she let go for more than one second.

It was ridiculous to want to hang on, when she was the one who had decided they needed to let go. And yet, here she was. Hanging on to him as though he were the only thing keeping her afloat in the storm.

Don't do this to yourself again.

Her heart was screaming at her. Six months. She had spent six months trying to get over Nico Katsaros and now she was going to fall willingly back into his arms? Back into his bed? She knew how this would go. There was no twist ending awaiting her.

But she couldn't resist. She never could. No, not from that first kiss all the way until this one. She had never been able to resist.

"One last time," he said against her mouth, his voice rough. "Give me this. Please."

"Why?" she whispered.

"So that I know it is the last time."

"What do you mean?"

"You surprised me with the divorce. I am certain that you knew the last time we made love would be the last time. But I did not."

Her face heated. Because she did know. She had been so acutely aware that she was saying goodbye to him the night before he left for that last business trip. She had known that she would be giving him the divorce papers when he returned. But he had no way of knowing that. She had known that last night that it was goodbye. And she had said it, with her body. Carried it with her even now.

"I didn't think you would care." She hadn't thought he would. Not for one second. She was surprised he hadn't replaced her in his bed already. She had never imagined she was special. She was just convenient.

"I care very much. And I am owed my goodbye."

She tried to squash the little bit of hope blooming in her chest. He cared about sex. He didn't care about her. His pride was likely wounded by her abandonment. Unsurprising, considering Nico was a very proud man.

And she wasn't nearly proud enough. Right now she felt needy, weak. Desperate for one more time.

"Then I'll give it to you. One last night."

He nodded once, his expression like stone. "One last night."

He broke their hold, his hand wrapping around hers as he led her from the dance floor. Every eye was on the masked couple as they broke through the crowd, moving quickly toward the lobby of the hotel.

Her heart was in her throat as they approached the front desk, and then, off to the left, she spotted a man in a suit. Tall, arresting.

Spencer Chatsfield.

Nico paused, then redirected their movements. "Hello, Mr. Chatsfield. We need a room for the night. Give us the best you have."

Spencer arched a brow, assessing them both, his expression carefully neutral. "Of course."

The moment Nico and Lucy were inside the elevator, the doors closed. Nico turned to her, pinning her against the wall, his hands on either side of her head. Restraint be damned. He had been nothing but patient. Nothing but restrained in the months since she had served him with divorce papers. Hadn't he given her everything she had demanded? Certainly, he had punished her by withholding her company from her, but she had broken her vows, and it was no less than she deserved.

Anger was once again penetrating the fog of lust that had descended over him. For a long time now, there had been only anger, blinding, white-hot anger. And now there was both. An intense need that was threatening to choke the life out of him combined with a kind of futile rage that he imagined one felt when they were watching the life's blood drain out of something precious. A kind of rage directed at the universe, a rage that had no recourse, no productivity. A rage that could fix nothing. A rage that could do nothing but simply be, filling up his entire being until he was driven by it, consumed by it.

He felt helpless in the face of it, and so, he dipped his head and consumed her. Poured all of it onto the woman who had caused it.

He broke the kiss, his lips still touching hers. "You have never done what I expected. You have never done what I asked."

She looked at him, glittering blue eyes filled with an anger that matched his own. "How can you say that? I was nothing but the perfect wife to you."

"You left me. And before that you tempted me. That was never a part of our bargain."

"I never tempted you. Temptation implies that it was something you wanted to resist. You demanded that I prove we have chemistry. And once we were married I was your business partner during the day and your whore at night. Nothing more. Never anything more. Don't you dare try and pretend I surprised you somehow. All I ever wanted was the business end of the arrangement. I never wanted this."

"You never wanted my kiss?"

"I never wanted to *need* it."

"And do you need it? Have you spent nights as I have? Aching, alone, desperate for something you know you can only have with the one person you can never touch again?"

She looked down. "I don't—"

He gripped her chin and forced her to look up at him. "Speak to me. Not to the floor."

"Yes," she said.

"I promise you one thing. After tonight you will burn for me forever."

By the time she and Nico entered the hotel room, she was shaking. His words were echoing in her mind.

After tonight you will burn for me forever.

She feared it was true. Because if the past few months were any indicator, she would never forget what it was like to be touched by him, kissed by him. She had a feeling that even if she went forward with life, filling up those empty spaces as best she could, there would always be one left vacant. Hollow. A space that could only ever be filled by Nico.

Nico sat on the edge of the mattress, leaning back, his thighs spread, the outline of his arousal clearly visible through his dark dress pants. Yes, she wanted him. Yes, she was going to have this. Even if it did make her burn. Forever and ever after. It would be worth it.

Just have him look at her like this again. To have him touch her again.

She reached up, ready to untie the mask that concealed part of her face.

"Leave it," he said, his words clipped, hard.

She lowered her hands. "And are you leaving yours?" she asked, looking at the slash of black leather still resting over his eyes.

"There is a certain appeal to it, don't you think? The opportunity to come together as strangers again. Perhaps we will learn new things, rather than simply assuming we already know them?"

She clung to part of his words, held them close to her chest. Strangers. Maybe if she could think of him as a stranger, this wouldn't hurt quite so much. Maybe she could get what she wanted from this without the pain.

She grabbed hold of the zipper tab on her dress, and slowly began to lower it. Letting her gown fall loose, leaving her standing there bare before her husband.

Nico took in the sight of his wife's body, her every delicious curve bared for his inspection. Only two things remained. Black panties that scarcely concealed anything, rather framing the part of herself he was most interested in. And the mask, a brilliant gold against her skin. His gift, unwrapped in all her glory.

Dark curls cascaded over her shoulders, her lips a crimson temptation.

He recalled the first time he had seen his wife, in her prim little business suits. He could never have imagined they would end up here. About to make love in a hotel room, wearing masks. On the brink of divorce.

He had a moment of feeling as though he were in someone else's life. A life not his own.

He'd had this woman. His wife. And he had somehow let her escape. Nico Katsaros, who failed at nothing. Who had dragged himself up from the bottom rung of society to the very top. And yet, it had not been enough. It had not been enough to keep his wife with him.

Had he not offered her everything? Money, security for her business, sex.

Somehow, as far as this woman was concerned, he was still not enough. He hated that feeling. Loathed it more than anything else on earth. He had spent all of his life being treated as though he was not enough, as though he was deficient because of his birth.

She had no right to treat him that way. Not now. No one did. He owned the world.

But you do not own her.

He gritted his teeth against that reminder. Perhaps not. Not in the grand scheme of things. But tonight he did.

"Come to me, Lucy. Give yourself to me," he said, each word a struggle.

She obeyed, moving nearer to him, pressing her knee into the mattress beside his thigh. "I thought we were strangers tonight?"

"If you please." He ran his thumb along the edge of her mask, then stretched up to kiss her mouth. "Show me what you like."

Lucy was shaking, her hands aching to touch, her body hollow with the need to be possessed by him. It was terrifying to need like this. This was why she had consented to marry Nico in the first place to save her father's ailing company. Because as far as she was concerned, a convenient marriage was the safest route to take. She didn't want to love, not again.

Everyone in her life she had loved, she had lost. Her mother had left before she was born, her father died far too soon...

She had never wanted to submit herself to that kind of pain again. That risk of loss.

It was why there had been no other men before Nico. She had avoided relationships, avoided attachments. She had imagined it would be easy to steer clear of emotional strings with a man like Nico. A man whose foundation was set upon business, his personal life built upon the sand, ever shifting and reshaping. He'd had a reputation as quite the playboy prior to their marriage. The sort of man women linked themselves to for an evening, but no more.

Foolish girl she had been, she had figured she would simply do the same. Connect herself physically with no emotional repercussions.

But she had been wrong. So very wrong.

He was right—she was keeping secrets from him. But it hadn't started that way.

Something had changed in her over the course of their marriage, taking root in her soul. Building, growing, until it had been almost impossible to hold back anymore. She had tried to deny it, not even allowing herself to think the words.

But they were there. Echoing through her all the same.

And as Nico rested his hand on her hip, dark eyes intent on her, she let them flow through her for the first time. Let her mind form them fully.

She had her secrets. But they were not the sorts of secrets he imagined.

Her deepest secret was that she had fallen in love with her husband.

Nico was thankful they were wearing the masks. Otherwise, he knew Lucy would be able to see the raw hunger

on his face. Would be able to see just how close he was
to losing control.

He moved his palm up from her hip, along the elegant
curve of her waist, to the full, brilliant temptation of her
breasts. A mere mask could never make them strangers,
though he appreciated the small barrier it provided. Still,
had he been wearing a blindfold he would've known it
was her. Would have known the particular softness of
her skin, the exact slope of the indent of her waist, just
where her breasts grew fuller.

He knew her body as well as he knew his own.

This was the last time.

That was the agreement.

Her hands went to his tie, delicate fingers slipping the
silk through the knot. He had forgotten the simple pleasure of having her undress him. The beauty in antici-
pating their coming together. Before their marriage he
had been with countless women, but from the moment
his lips had touched hers, he had never wanted another.

Slowly, she slipped her fingertips inside his shirt, her
palm resting over his raging heartbeat.

He lifted his gaze from her beautiful body to her eyes.
She was trying to hide too. Trying to use the mask to
conceal how she felt in the intensity of this moment.
He raised his own hand, placed it over hers, trapping it
against his skin. Then he closed the distance between
them and kissed her.

Lucy made quick work of her husband's clothes, repeat-
ing actions she had carried out hundreds of times before.
But this was different. Final. It made her ache.

She drank in the sight of him. His broad shoulders
and chest, sprinkled with just the right amount of chest

hair. His well-defined abs that shifted and rippled with each indrawn breath. And of course, the most male part of him, the part of him that she was desperate for now.

She memorized every detail. The flex of his thighs, the way his fingers curled around the bedspread, the gold wedding band he still wore bright against his dark skin, the tendons in the backs of his hands standing out as he fought to anchor himself to the bed.

She straddled his lap, kissing him deeply as she pressed her breasts against him. It was sexual, there was no denying it, but there was also something deeply emotional about being close to him like this again. Being skin to skin.

She had, after years of it, taken such intimacy for granted. Had been certain it hadn't been intimacy at all. But now that she had been living without him, she knew that hadn't been true. Recognized that there had been more emotion when they'd touched than she had begun to imagine. Empty, she had allowed herself to believe it was empty.

Now she felt that evaluation may have been unfair.

"Have you continued to take your contraceptive pill?" he asked, his voice rough, strained.

He was as near the edge as she was, and she found it immensely gratifying.

She nodded, because speech was beyond. His mouth went slightly slack, abject relief visible on his face even with some of his features obscured by the mask.

He wrapped his arm around her waist, moving his hand down to cup her rear, and at the same time sweeping her panties to the side. She shifted her position, and allowed him to slide deep inside of her.

Tears stung the backs of her eyes, and she shut them tight to try to keep them back.

How had she ever thought this was empty?

This was the last time. And she feared that without Nico, she would never be anything but empty ever again.

He was surrounded by her, lost in her. The feel of her, the scent of her. He reached up, sifting his fingers through her silky curtain of dark curls, relishing the sensation. He flexed his hips, sliding deeper inside the damp heat of her body.

He had thought their first time, five years ago, was powerful. But it was nothing in comparison to this. Because in their first time had been the promise of forever, while this was the promise of an end. And with that came the desperation to make it count, to make it last. To make sure she would burn, forever.

Because he would.

He grabbed hold of her bottom, moving into a standing position, wrapping her legs around his waist, keeping himself buried deep inside of her. He turned and lowered her back to the bed, reversing their positions and thrusting down inside of her.

He was as deep in her as he could possibly get, and it wasn't enough. It would never be enough.

She gasped, arching against him, and he captured the sound with his mouth, kissing her as he allowed himself to get lost in the rhythm of their bodies. Lost in her.

Soon, too soon, his climax rushed up to meet him, overtaking him like a savage beast, grabbing him by the throat and shaking him hard, leaving pleasure to bleed out through his body in an unstoppable tide. He gritted his teeth and thrust into her one last time, grinding against the bundle of nerves at the apex of her thighs, holding position until she made the sweet familiar sound of release, her internal muscles tightening around him.

He didn't move, not for a long while. Her red lips parted, a long sigh escaping.

And then a single tear tracked from beneath her golden mask and slid down her cheek, leaving a dark blot on the pillowcase.

"Lucy?" he asked, moving away from her.

She shook her head. "No. No names. Please. Please let's be strangers."

Lucy was gasping for breath, a haze of pleasure tangling with the sharp, keen clarity of what she had just done. Of the fact that it was over.

He started to get up, as was his routine after they made love. For all five years of their marriage, they would make love and he would leave, go back to his own room, leave her there with nothing more than his scent on her pillow to keep her company as her sheets cooled.

She couldn't stand that right now. Just this once, she needed him to stay.

"Don't go."

He paused. "But you're upset."

"No. Yes," she said, laughing slightly while she wiped the moisture from her cheeks. "I don't know what I am. But I don't want to be alone."

"You like to be left alone. After we…"

"What made you think that?"

"You prize your space, Lucy. I have always tried to respect that. You made it very plain when we were first married that you wanted to sleep alone."

His words hit her like a brick. They weren't wrong.

She had made a very big deal about wanting to preserve her space. But that was before they were married. Certainly before they had shared years of intimacy. Surely, he must have known that she would want him to stay.

"I didn't always want space," she said.

"When? When did it change?"

She knew when. But she didn't want to tell him.

"We were strangers when we first married. Of course, after we got to know each other. After it was more than just physical… I suppose I never told you."

"No."

"I wished you would stay." So much easier to tell him these things while she was wearing the mask. While she was pretending they were just strangers, talking. Yes, they were talking about a shared past, but somehow the game, the idea, allowed her the distance she needed to speak to him without falling apart.

"I would have liked that," he said, his voice rough.

"We kept too many secrets."

Dark eyes met hers, and he moved nearer to her again. "Did we? What were yours? Tell me your secrets, *agape*."

Nico watched the pulse beat hard at the base of her neck, watched as the delicate color leached from her cheeks. She was so beautiful. He had always thought so. But he didn't know if he had ever *felt* it.

He felt it now. Echoing in his soul, reverberating down deep in his bones. The kind of beauty you didn't just witness, but the kind that took up residence inside you. Changed you. How had he been blind to it until he had lost it?

"You don't want to know about me," she said, her voice soft.

"There will never be another chance for me to learn. And we are just strangers. So tell me. Tell me who you are. Then, when we leave here, perhaps we will not be strangers. Though, we will not meet again," he said.

"You know everything there is to know about me."

"No, I don't. Because we are strangers. Talk to me like I am a stranger, and not your husband. And I daresay I will learn more in that conversation than any we have had in the past five years." He didn't know why he was making the demand, didn't know why it suddenly seemed so important. Only that it did.

She shifted her position, rolling to her side, and he watched her breasts move with her. Completely captivated, but not only by her body—by the words she would speak next. "All right. You know my mother left. And that it was just me and my father. And I wanted… I wanted so badly to please him. And I did. I poured everything that I was into learning about Kennewick, into helping him with ideas. I wanted to be involved in it so that we would have something in common. And he loved sharing all of that with me. And then he died. And Kennewick was all I had. By the time you and I met… I felt as though everything that I had ever cared about I was destined to lose. So that's why I couldn't find someone to be my maid of honor at the wedding. And that's why there were no men before you. Because earning the love of the only family member I had left meant pouring everything into the company. And I did love Kennewick. But you can love a business, and you can love the money it brings in. But it can never love you back." She took a deep breath. "Finally, I realized that. I realized that no amount of pouring into it would replicate the love I had lost when my father died. And so, I decided I was tired of pouring in and getting nothing back. I decided I was tired of being empty."

"You felt... Empty? Even when you were with me?"

She lifted a bare shoulder. "Sometimes being skin to skin with someone and knowing they don't care for you is even more devastating than simply being alone." She pushed herself into a sitting position, drawing her knees up to her chest. "Now...tell me your secrets."

Lucy watched, waited to see if he would turn away from her, or if he would share. She wanted him to tell her, wanted to tear down that wall that he kept between himself and the world, himself and her, and finally understand the man she had shared her life with for half a decade. Of course, it wasn't fair. Because she had talked of familial love, and manufacturing companies, and never once spoken of the fact that what had truly left her feeling empty was loving him when she knew he didn't love her back.

"I was the bastard son of a poor woman. I worked hard, got straight A's in school, got scholarships, worked my way from the ground up at one of the largest national conglomerates... But you can find all this out by reading my bio."

"But we are sharing. As though we're strangers," she said. "What inspired you to work hard? What inspired you to change?"

There was a slight pause. "I saw opulence all around me every day, and yet I was not allowed to partake in it. I vowed that I would have my own piece of that opulence someday. I was so tired of being denied."

It was easy then, to imagine him as a small boy, surrounded by the luxuries of the world while constantly being told they were off-limits. How confusing it must have been.

"You must be proud. Of everything you have achieved."

"Typically. Typically, I am. And yet, I find myself being denied again. I don't like it, Lucy. I don't like it one bit."

"What have you been denied?"

His dark eyes blazed into hers. "You."

Her heart leaped against her breastbone. "Find another wife. It won't be difficult for you."

"But it's you that I want. I want you."

"Why? Because I matter? Because you're still a small boy throwing a tantrum over the things you can't have?"

A feral growl escaped his lips, and she found herself pinned against the mattress, Nico above her, his expression fierce. And for the first time that night, he reached up and tore off the mask.

"Am I a boy? I think not. Perhaps you need me to show you again that I am in fact very much a man."

"Why would you need to show me?" she asked, desperation pouring through her. "Why should you care?"

"Do not forget that you are the one who demanded to divorce, *agape*. Not me. I did not want this. I never wanted it."

"Why?" she asked, ferocity lacing her tone. "You haven't given me a satisfactory answer to my question."

He growled, flexing his hips, giving her a taste of his growing arousal, and in spite of herself, her body responded. "Is this not answer enough?"

"No. You have always acted like it should be enough. It isn't enough."

"Why not? I gave you my name. I gave you my money. I saved your failing business. I gave you my home. A place in my bed. And you reject me. You tell me I'm not enough. I made vows to you, and still I am not enough."

"Because you didn't give me what I wanted."

"You have never told me what you wanted," he said, desperation filling his tone now, matching her own. "You didn't tell me you wanted to share my bed all night. You didn't tell me you wanted to share a room. You kept these things from me, and then you punished me for not guessing what you never spoke out loud."

There was no response she could give to that. Because he was right. She had never told him what she wanted. Had never told him what she felt, that she was empty, that she was desperate for more from him. She hadn't told him that she loved him. She had been consumed with protecting herself, with preventing another loss. So she had run, not realizing the fatal flaw in her plan. She already loved him, so whether or not she told him, whether or not she ever gave him the chance to reject her, she would lose him if she ran.

But she didn't know if she was brave enough to stay. Didn't know if she was brave enough to speak those words to him, to watch his face change. To one of horror, of pity. He didn't want love; he had stated it plainly. Had told her explicitly after their wedding that theirs would never be a union held together by emotion.

So she had believed him.

What you wanted changed. Perhaps what he wanted has changed too. But you will never know, because you are a coward.

It was true. She was.

And it had to stop.

She curled her fingers around her mask and pulled it away. And they were Nico and Lucy again. There was no more hiding. She refused to hide anymore.

"I still haven't told you my last secret."

Nico looked down at his wife, her eyes glittering with emotion, and he felt his rage drain away. He moved away from her, pushing himself into a sitting position and forking his fingers through his hair. "I'm sorry, Lucy."

He heard the rustle of the covers as she sat up, felt the light touch of her fingertips against his shoulder. "Do you want to hear my secret?"

His chest seized up tight. "Is it fair to say that I'm not sure?"

"I suppose so. Since I'm not sure I want to tell it. But I realized that all of the silence between us is what broke things. So I doubt there's anything I could say now that would make it worse."

"We are getting divorced the day after tomorrow. It doesn't get worse than that."

She laughed softly, her breath fanning over his bare skin. "I suppose so." Still, she said nothing. She only moved nearer to him, pressed her body against him, holding him.

"You're stalling, *agape*."

"You always call me that," she said, her voice soft.

"I suppose I do."

"From the beginning. You've always called me that."

Discomfort crawled over his skin. "Yes. It is a common endearment."

"It means *love*."

"I'm well aware of the meaning."

"I used to find it slightly annoying. I mean at first.

Because it was all a charade, and neither you nor I were pretending to have any finer feelings. But one day...one day you said it and everything sort of slowed down. And I realized that whether or not you meant anything when you called me that it meant something to me. Because, Nico, I love you."

Heat and cold rushed through Nico's body, a reaction he could not have anticipated.

But then, his wife's words were nothing he could have ever anticipated. She loved him? And she was telling him this two nights before their divorce was final.

He turned to look at the clock. After midnight. Not even two nights until their divorce was final. It was Christmas now.

He stood, collecting his clothes and putting them on as quickly as possible. He was aware of Lucy watching him, but he didn't look at her. He couldn't look at her. He was too lost in the feelings riding through him. Anger. Pain. But most of all, fear.

It was the fear that won.

"Our last night together has come to an end," he said, keeping his eyes fixed on a place on the wall behind her. "Merry Christmas, Lucy."

And then he turned and walked out the door.

It was a truly vile Christmas, thank you very much. No matter how resolutely the radio played music proclaiming it a merry one, Lucy simply couldn't feel it.

She had done it. She had told him. Confessed all, and he had rejected her. No, he had not even had the decency to reject her. He had simply walked out. With nary anything but a season's greeting.

She should feel vindicated. Obviously, she had been

right asking for the divorce. Obviously, no amount, or lack, of communication could have possibly altered the course of their relationship. She had changed, what she wanted had changed, but what he wanted hadn't.

Certainly, he had been more than willing to have sex with her, but that was no indication of any finer feelings. Typical.

She took a sip of wine, then set her glass back down on the sideboard in the living room. The crystal made contact with the wood surface with a resounding click, echoing against the walls of her family home. Highlighting the fact that she was truly alone.

Here she was, living the exact thing she had been afraid of. Loving again. Losing it again.

The only positive thing she could say was that she was living. For now, she would take it.

The doorbell rang, and she crossed the expansive living area, heading toward the entry. If it was carolers, she could not promise she wouldn't throw them in a snowbank. She wasn't feeling particularly cheered, and she didn't really want anyone to try.

She paused at the door and looked through the security glass. And then her heart stopped. There were no Dickensian street urchins, no carolers of any kind.

It was Nico.

She opened the door to the town house, her sadness suddenly washed away by a torrent of anger. "What do you want? You didn't hurt me enough last night? Have you also come to step on my toe? Get a red wine stain on the cream-colored rug? Or perhaps something else similarly damaging?"

"No," he said, his voice ragged. For the first time, she paused and looked at him, really looked. And she noticed he appeared as though he had not slept since he had left her in the hotel room. "I came here because I have one more secret to tell you."

The last time Nico had felt so nervous, he had knocked over a vase in the hallowed halls of the home his mother had worked in. He had known then, though he had been only a child, that he had broken something priceless. That there would be no fixing it. That the only way out would be if those he had wronged forgave his debt, because there was no way he could pay it.

It was the same as this moment. He had broken something last night. Perhaps he had been steadily breaking it over the past five years. He wasn't sure there was any way to fix it. And so, instead he would ask for forgiveness. And offer something in return.

"Tell me," Lucy said, her voice thin.

"I hated Christmas as a child. It was so happy and warm. It was everything I was not. A display of all I could not have. It made me want. It made me feel. It made me ache. To be tantalized by all that you cannot have from your very earliest memory... There was a point where I decided I would never do that again. I would no longer want—I would have. And I would do what needed to be done to obtain the means to make it possible. Then I met you. And I... I acquired you. As I have done many things in the past."

"I'm not certain I find that flattering."

"It isn't. Simply the reasoning of a frightened man." He drew a deep breath. "We were married for five years. And I never once brought a Christmas tree or anything festive at all into our house, did I?"

"No," she said.

"It is because I didn't want to ache anymore. Reminders of the past…of that longing… They only made me ache and so I kept them away. But I couldn't stop that pain forever."

"You couldn't?"

"No. Because of you. You are my Christmas, Lucy Kennewick."

"I'm your what?"

"You are my Christmas. Being near you, so close to you, and yet not having you made me ache. So I pretended I didn't need you. I pretended you weren't important. When in truth all I really wanted was one moment of the warmth, of the happiness, I knew I could find in you." He cleared his throat. "But I was afraid. Afraid of wanting something I might not be able to have. You were right, in many ways. I am just a boy afraid of being denied."

Lucy felt as though her heart was going to explode. She stepped out the door, wrapping her arms around Nico, squeezing her eyes shut tight. "Oh, Nico. You don't have to be afraid of me. You don't have to be afraid of not having me."

"When you asked for your divorce… I told myself I hated you. Because yet again I was being denied. So I decided I wouldn't think of you. I wouldn't remember you. I wouldn't want you. Because it was better than the pain." He looked away. "Of course… I could not let go entirely. It's why I wore the ring still. Because I didn't want it to be over, no matter what I told myself."

"I hurt you? Believe me when I tell you I had no clue I possessed the power to hurt you."

He drew back slightly, his dark eyes trained on hers. "I didn't know either. Because I worked so hard to ensure that nothing did. But you…you got beneath my defenses. You were so unexpected. A virgin in business suits who wanted a marriage of convenience. Why should I ever think I would have to protect my heart from such a creature?"

She frowned. "I am not a creature."

He leaned in and kissed her lips lightly. "Of course not."

"So what do you…? I mean… How do you feel about Christmas now?" she asked, her heart thundering heavily.

"I assume by Christmas you mean you."

"That is the metaphor."

A smile curved his lips. "Aren't you going to invite me in?"

Nico had spent the whole night wandering the city feeling tortured. Feeling as though his heart had been ripped straight out of his chest and hung up on a tree in Rockefeller Center as a macabre ornament.

And then he had asked himself what the hell he was doing, wandering the city streets in the cold when he could be with his wife. When there was a woman who loved him. A woman he knew beyond a shadow of a doubt he wanted to spend the rest of his life with.

So, he had come to her.

"I would invite you in," she said, blocking the door with her petite frame. "But there are Christmas decorations in there. And I'm not sure yet how you feel about those."

"I love them," he said, the words rough, torn from him.

Her lips went slack, rounded into an O. "You do?"

"Yes."

"Why…why did you never tell Christmas? And why

did you let Christmas almost divorce you? And why did you walk out of the hotel room without saying anything when Christmas confessed its true feelings?"

"Because," he said, tugging Lucy into his arms and kissing her hard. "Because I am little more than a frightened boy. I had aspirations. I wanted things. But, Lucy, that's nothing compared to risking your heart. I didn't want to let anything or anyone hurt me, ever again. I married you because you were safe. But then it turned out you weren't. So I kept you at a distance and…and then you left me. Lucy, these past six months without you have been hell."

"They have been," she said. "I mean, for me too. Without you."

"I know I don't ever want to lose you again. And I know that means investing more than I have. I know that means giving. I know that means opening up. It means risking pain."

"But healing too," she said, tears filling her eyes. "And happiness. And love. Lots of love."

He kissed her again. "I know. It's worth the risk. And now you know my secrets. If I ever close up, if I ever turn away…"

"I'll ask you why. And you do the same for me."

"I promise."

"I love you, Nico."

His heart expanded in his chest. "I love you too, Lucy. Stay my wife. Please."

"I will." She kissed him again and he looked beyond her, through the door and at the house inside. He could see a Christmas tree, lights twinkling everywhere. And he knew for a fact Christmas would never again be a promise not kept.

It would be, for him, the ultimate symbol of vows honored.

"Now maybe you should come inside," she said, a smile on her face. "I have a present for you that you might want to unwrap."

* * * * *

#3397 AWAKENING THE RAVENSDALE HEIRESS
The Ravensdale Scandals
by Melanie Milburne

Miranda Ravensdale's first love ended in tragedy, so she vowed to bury her heart with the memories. No man has broken through her facade—until billionaire Leandro Allegretti! Leandro plans to coax her dormant sensuality into life, kiss by seductive kiss...

#3398 WEARING THE DE ANGELIS RING
The Italian Titans
by Cathy Williams

Tycoon Theo De Angelis lives by his own rules...until a family debt forces him into matrimony! Beautiful, inexperienced Alexa Caldini is determined to impose ground rules on their inconvenient arrangement, but how long before Alexa's rules go up in smoke?

#3399 THE MARRIAGE HE MUST KEEP
The Wrong Heirs
by Dani Collins

Alessandro Ferrante was pleasantly surprised to discover passion in his convenient marriage to shy heiress Octavia. But when their fragile union is tested, Alessandro *must* seduce his wife again and ensure Octavia—and his child—are his forever!

#3400 MISTRESS OF HIS REVENGE
Bought by the Brazilian
by Chantelle Shaw

Cruz Delgado is the renowned owner of a diamond empire—and aristocratic Sabrina Bancroft is the *only* woman ever to have walked away from the tempting tycoon. When Cruz sees a chance, he takes his revenge...by making her his mistress!

YOU CAN FIND MORE INFORMATION ON UPCOMING HARLEQUIN® TITLES, FREE EXCERPTS AND MORE AT WWW.HARLEQUIN.COM.

HPCNM1215RB

REQUEST YOUR FREE BOOKS!

*Can King Kairos claim his heir and convince his
beautiful queen Tabitha that they're bound by duty,
passion and love, before the clock strikes midnight on
their fairy tale?*

Read on for a sneak preview of
THE QUEEN'S NEW YEAR SECRET,
the final book in **Maisey Yates**'s *sensational duet*
PRINCES OF PETRAS.

"I don't think we've ever…really been alone before."

"We are very often alone," he said, frowning.

"In a palace filled with hundreds, in a building other
people live in."

"I have never kidnapped you before, either. You've
also never been pregnant with my baby. Oh, yes, and we
have never been on the brink of divorce. So, a season of
firsts. How nice to add this to the list."

She stood up, stretching out her stiff muscles. "Where
exactly do you get off being angry at me? We are here
because of you."

"I'm angry with you because this divorce is happening
at your demand."

"Had I not demanded we divorce, I wouldn't be pregnant."

"Had you not frozen me out of your bed, perhaps you
would have been pregnant a couple of months sooner."

She gritted her teeth, reckless heat pouring through her veins. "How dare you?" She advanced on him, and he wrapped his arm around her waist, pulling her close. "Don't."

Her protest was cut off by the press of his mouth against hers, hot and uncompromising, his tongue staking a claim as he took her deep, hard. She had no idea where these kinds of kisses had come from. Who this man was. This man who would spirit her away to a private island. Who kissed her like he was a dying man and her lips held his salvation.

He kissed her neck, down to her collarbone, retracing that same path with the tip of his tongue. She found herself tearing at his shirt, her heart thundering hard, every fiber of her being desperate to have him. Desperate to have him inside her again. Like that night in his office. That night when the promise that had been broken on their wedding night was finally fulfilled.

Don't miss
THE QUEEN'S NEW YEAR SECRET by Maisey Yates,
available January 2016 wherever
Harlequin Presents® books and ebooks are sold.

www.Harlequin.com

HPEXP1215